DRAECUS CLAN BOOK 1

DRAGON TAKEN

ALEXIS PIERCE

Every girl dreams of waking up one day, a princess. Until that day kicks you in the face, wearing steel toed boots.
L.A. Kennedy

CHAPTER ONE
SERENITY

I sneer at my phone. I cannot believe that Mom and Dad just bought Adam a condo. A freaking condo!

Meanwhile, I'm still working in the media lab in the basement of a run-down university I hadn't even heard of until I saw the application. The job barely covers rent in my shared three-bedroom, and my bedroom is basically a closet. Well, it is a closet. Converted into a "charming" bedroom. This is not what I needed to find out the day before my rent is due.

Tears spring to my eyes. This is the final straw.

My hands grow hot, and I have to take a deep breath to calm the unexplainable heat that always appears every time I get angry.

I hit the call button, and, before she can answer, I say, "Mom, what the hell?"

A sigh comes out on the other end, but she doesn't explain. I have been treated as lesser than my brother since he was born. I was five, and I suddenly knew exactly what it felt like to be unloved. The tears begin to fall, and I have to lean back so they don't hit the keyboard of the department's ancient desktop.

"I know I'm not as smart as Adam, or as successful as Adam, but—"

Before I can ramp up into a whole long rant, she cuts me off. "Serenity, it's not that." Her tone is sharp, a whip cutting through my voice. I am effectively silenced. "It's just that your well-being isn't as much of a priority to us right now."

Or ever, I don't add. Instead, I just whisper, "Why?" as another tear splashes down on the list of tasks I have to complete before the end of my shift. I have to know. Why don't I matter as much? Is it because I'm a girl? Is it because I'm not very smart? Why, why, *why*?

I can practically hear Mom chewing her lip, something she does when she's particularly nervous. It's a habit she would never do in public, but something she always seems to perform in front of me. "Fine," she says. "*Fine*. Your father didn't want me to tell you this, but he's out on business right now, and I'm sick of your constant whining. When you were a baby, he went to Russia and adopted you without my knowing. He thought we would never have a baby. And then we were pretty much stuck with you, so I didn't complain, even though you've been nothing but trouble."

All my words dry up. I know about the trouble, of course. The bad grades. The mysterious, unexplainable disasters. Not to mention the time I got caught having sex in a supply closet in high school. That one was particularly egregious. My parents have spent years covering up my messes, but still. Russia? It's not possible. How in the world could they keep something like this from me? "You're lying," I croak, but I can hear it in her cold, hard voice. It explains everything. Every moment of disdain, every ounce of cruelty she's ever dished out. She doesn't love me. Hell, she doesn't even like me.

Before she can continue, I hang up the phone.

I just can't deal with this today. Why would she say something like that? I must be dreaming.

I shake my head, pinch my arm, snap the rubber ponytail holder on my wrist, but it does nothing. No, this is real. Very, very real. I wrap my arms around myself and tremble. After a brief breakdown, though, I get back to work. Rent isn't gonna pay itself.

When my night shift ends, I tuck my long blonde hair up under a pale pink beanie, then wrap myself in the cheap coat I bought last year. It has a few holes in it, but otherwise, it's been good enough to keep me alive in the otherwise deadly New York City winters.

My phone buzzes in my pocket, and I pull it out to see Dad's image on the screen. I hit ignore and prepare to walk home. My Metro card expired last month, and I haven't had enough money to get a new one. Even a week-long one is expensive as hell. I keep telling myself I'll get it with my next paycheck, but that was three checks ago. Oh, well. It's only fifteen blocks in the snow.

As I pass the front desk, the college student working it waves me over. What could possibly be happening now?

"Mr. Thompson wants to speak with you," she says, not even deigning to look at me.

I suppress a groan and go to the dingy office behind her. Mr. Thompson is an older man, his mouth set in a permanent frown. The way he looks at me, eyes tracing slowly over my body like I'm a piece of cake he wants to eat, sends a shiver through me. As I'm about to sit on the ratty yellowed couch—did it use to be white?—he shakes his head. "This won't take long."

My heart speeds up, and a lump forms in my throat. His frown appears to set even deeper. "Your job performance has been less than optimal lately, Ms. Fuoco. Which is why the department has decided to let you go."

I bite my lip, but all I can do is nod. I will not cry in front of this man. I will not break. I will wait until I get home, hidden behind my bedroom door. *Closet door*, my unhelpful brain corrects.

"That's all. Have a good day."

I know exactly what this is. It has nothing to do with my job performance and everything to do with the fact that I wouldn't sleep with him when he came onto me two days ago. Honestly, it had taken all the self-control I had not to punch him in the dick when it happened.

I turn around and walk out of the building, heart slowing to a crawl. It's almost like I'm in a trance. The snow doesn't crunch underfoot, and there aren't any cars or people around. The city that never sleeps seems to have abandoned me, just like everyone else.

A scuffle catches my ears as I pass an alleyway, and I turn my head, hesitating. My hands warm defensively, but I clench them into fists. Not here. I can't have one of my episodes in front of a stranger. What if they told people? What if I were found out?

I grit my teeth.

"Serenity?" a voice calls. I tilt my head. Is it someone I know? I squint, but I don't make out more than a vague shadow. The voice is marginally familiar, but I can't quite place it. Maybe if I could see their face.

I look around, but there's nobody else on the snowy street. It's the first snowfall of the season, and the citizens of this neighborhood seem to have abandoned the already dark night for the warmth of their homes or jobs. The only person I can see is a man standing in the bodega across the street, his back turned to me. A tingle runs up my spine, and the hairs on the back of my neck stand on end.

"Serenity," the voice says again, more impatiently this time.

Right. "Who is it? I can't see you." I squint into the darkness, but it doesn't help. I fumble for the phone in my pocket. I could use the flashlight.

Instead, though, it falls out of my hand. "Sorry," I say with a nervous laugh. "It's really not my night."

As I bend over to pick up the device, the voice gets so much closer. "No, it's not."

Before I can scream, a piece of fabric is shoved in my mouth, and my arms are pinned to my sides.

CHAPTER TWO
ADRIAN

I'm not totally sure it's her at first. For one, she's bundled in a black coat, her hair hidden by a pink knit beanie. When she turns to me, though, her eyes are an icy blue that bore into me from all the way across the street. I quickly turn my back to her. If I'm right, who knows what she could do to me? What powers could she contain in such an unassuming form?

When it's been long enough, and her gaze slides off me, I turn around to evaluate her some more.

Instead of finding her looking around the

street, though, she's gone. I stumble out of the bodega and into the snow. I can't transform here, though. Too many possible witnesses. I suck in a deep breath through my nose. She's still close. I glance around and let my eyes change. Instead of being dark brown, any bystander would be able to see the now molten gold with slit pupils. I walk over carefully—I didn't bring backup. Perhaps I should have waited for more to arrive, but another sniff reveals the truth.

The girl is afraid. Terrified. Her aura hits me like a punch to the gut.

I squint into the alleyway, and my eyes focus on a masked figure dragging her back by a rope around her neck. Fury rips through me, and my hands catch fire instantly. Nobody touches her like that. I sprint into the darkness, grabbing ahold of the man's arm and ripping it away from the young woman. As soon as she's free, she rips the gag out of her mouth.

"Run," I gasp, my control wavering as her aura washes over me. Fear. Grief. I grit my teeth when she doesn't leave. "Now," I bark. She startles and sprints away. I will find her later. After all, she is my queen. There is nothing in the world that could keep me from finding her now that I've caught her scent.

As soon as she turns the corner, I refocus on the man screeching in front of me. I cover his mouth with a palm, but I don't relax the fiery grip melting the skin on his wrist. I do, however, turn down the heat just a bit.

"Who sent you?" I hiss.

He shakes his head, and tears pour out of his eyes, the only part of his face I can decipher.

I grimace. I didn't want to have to do this, but if he won't be speaking anyway, I must.

I just hope that nobody comes running when they hear his neck snap.

CHAPTER THREE
SERENITY

My hands shake, and I drop my keys twice before I can unlock the door to my apartment. I run inside, and the place is pitch black. I vaguely remember something about a comedy show with today's date on the flyer. *Fuck.* Greg is gonna be pissed that I missed his show. At least I have a pretty good excuse. After tossing my coat on the rack by the door, I sink down onto the couch just as the buzzer rings. I groan. Why can't I just be alone? I've been through a lot today.

I walk over to the door and click the button, and a man's face pops up, gray and pixelated on the little viewing screen. Still, I can't mistake the mysterious man who saved me from the alleyway. A shiver runs up my spine when he looks into the camera. It's almost like he can see me, but that's ridiculous.

"What?" I ask in my most authoritative New Yorker voice possible. Still, the little word shakes.

"You dropped your wallet," the man says, his voice deep and husky and gentler than I could imagine from such an imposing figure. He has an accent that I can't quite place. Italian, maybe? That's not quite it. I sigh. I guess I'll have to go downstairs. He did save me, right? So how much of a threat could he be? Still, I grab a cleaver from Greg's forbidden special knife block and tuck it into the back pocket of my jeans. Not risking anything else tonight.

"I'll be down in a minute," I say. No way am I letting that man in my apartment.

He shakes his head. "Serenity, I need to speak with you. It's about your parents."

That makes me hesitate. "You know my parents?"

He nods, and his next words turn me to ice. "Your birth parents."

I hadn't even known I was adopted until today. How does this total stranger know about it?

Does he know my mother? Well, adopted mother. A shiver runs through me, and it has nothing to do with the cold. I click the button, and he smiles gently before the screen goes black. What the hell am I getting myself into?

He's a lot taller than I remember from the alleyway. Perhaps it's because he'd been stooped over, his hand wrapped around my attacker's arm. His hand that had been—

I shake my head. It's not possible. People's hands don't just catch fire. I shake my hands out as they heat in protest. *Most people's hands don't catch fire*, I tell my rebellious brain.

When he removes his hood, which is sprinkled with snow, his full face comes into view, and I bite my lip. His skin is tanned and his short hair is rough, but his eyes are gentle and dark and so sad that I could break down crying right here and now. I wrap my arms around myself.

"Who are you?" I ask, my determination gone with one look at his face. He runs a hand over his pale facial hair in thought. His hair is either light brown or dark blonde, and I'm tempted to tangle my fingers in it. I clench my hands against me. What is wrong with me tonight? Other than exhaustion—mental and physical.

He takes a bow. An actual bow. Like something out of a movie.

"Adrian Byrne," he says. I laugh nervously at the absurdity of the moment. This guy can't be serious. Did I invite a New York weirdo into my apartment?

"Okaaaay," I say, drawing out the word and taking a step back from him. "And what do you know about my birth parents, Adrian Byrne?" I'm skeptical once again. This time, though, I refuse to melt into his chocolaty eyes when they meet mine. I'm home alone with a random stranger, so I can't let my guard down. Not for a moment.

"What do you know of your heritage?" he asks, walking further into my apartment. I clutch the knife in my pocket, watching him evaluate the space.

"I know I was born in Russia," I offer hesitantly.

He nods. "That makes sense. Russia is so far from the island. It's a smart place to hide you."

I open my mouth, close it, then open it again. I probably look like a fish, but he's too busy looking at one of the paintings on the wall, something that Jenna, my other roommate, bought at an estate sale and insists is worth some real money. Adrian removes his coat and lays it over one arm, revealing temptingly toned muscles. "Island?" I ask, forcing my eyes to his face.

He doesn't even look at me, just nods. "Draecus Island. Where my people—your people—are from."

I frown. "Never heard of it."

He smiles. "Of course not. That's because it's protected by magic."

I let out another laugh, this one harsh and far too loud for the small, empty apartment. "Magic. Right."

He turns his head to me, but he doesn't move otherwise. His eyebrows crease together, and my fingers itch to smooth out that spot on his forehead. "Surely you can't find that to be a ridiculous thought. You must have some sort of powers. Even if you are bound, it's impossible to contain a dragon's fire for this long undetected."

My smile fades, but I'm stuck on one word. "Dragon? Right. Okay. I'll let my mermaid friends know."

He frowns, the lines making him appear less gentle and more like some sort of ancient warrior. "I assure you, this is no laughing matter." His face shifts, just a little, becomes sharper. Then, right in front of me, his eyes turn gold, like a cat's, and his fingers sharpen into claws.

This can't be real. I've had a traumatic evening. Nausea roils through me, and I run to the sink, vomiting up my potato chip dinner from an hour ago. An easygoing hand gathers my hair, pulling it away from my face. I have to be seeing things. Imagining it. Dreaming? Yes, dreaming.

"You'll be alright, Serenity," he says. I don't dare look at him, but I don't pull away from his touch, either. "It can be a shock if you aren't aware."

I should be embarrassed at Adrian seeing me throwing up in my kitchen sink, but he rubs a hand gently over my back, and I just want to lean into his fiery touch.

Another buzz rings, and he jerks away from me.

"They've found you," he breathes. I rinse my mouth out and look at the door, then at him. His eyebrows are bunched together with concern, and his eyes are still that gold color.

"It's probably just the mail," I say, but he looks like a trapped animal, his eyes crazed when he turns his attention back on me.

"Is there a back way out of here? A fire escape, perhaps? Anything?"

I clench my hands and nod.

"We have to leave," he says. "Now. It's not safe for you in New York any longer. It's lucky I found you when I did, or you would be lost to us already." He paces over to me and wraps his large, hot hand around my smaller one. The claws are gone, I note with relief, and his eyes turn back to normal. "I know you have no reason to trust me, but I need you to come with me right now."

I look back at the door when the buzzer goes off again. "Where would you take me?"

He pulls me closer to him. We're almost touching now. The heat radiates off him, and he smells incredible. Is that sandalwood? "Somewhere safe. Somewhere they can't get you."

I swallow. "Is it the man from earlier?"

He doesn't answer, but I can see it in the look in his eyes. No, of course not. That particular man isn't a threat anymore.

This is nuts, right? I'm about to run away with a guy I just met today. A guy who might have killed somebody this very evening.

When a fist pounds at the door, I nod. "Okay," I say. "I'll trust you. But I'm warning you, I have a knife." The metal digs in the back pocket of my jeans, reminding me of its comforting presence. I may not have any fighting skills, but at least I have something.

He cracks a tense smile. "And I pray you won't need to use it."

CHAPTER FOUR
MATTHEW

I pace the living room, running my hands through my chest-length dark hair. Why is nobody else worried? Adrian should be back by now. This was just a normal recon mission. Another supposed sighting of the woman who's supposed to magically solve all our problems.

Yeah, right.

"Matthew, you need to calm down," Dylan says. He's just lounging on the sofa playing video games. He doesn't even care.

"Aren't you the least bit concerned?" I demand, slamming my hands on the marble countertop that separates the kitchen from the living area.

"Don't break the house," Liam says from the stove. He's always cooking something, and, when he's nervous, he's usually baking. I glance at him, and he's pouring brownie mix into a pan. So I'm not the only one who's freaking out. When I turn back to Dylan to confront him, though, he's glancing at his phone nervously. They may seem nonchalant, but they're both secretly freaking out. Good.

"I'm going to bed," I announce. I go upstairs so the others don't see me panicking. I've known Adrian longer than anyone, and he's never been late to anything before. Where the hell is he? My mind runs through worst-case scenarios as I watch the lazy snow fall through the sprawling upstate property. The night is far too peaceful for the way I feel right now. My stomach rolls, and I think I might be sick if he doesn't show up soon. "Where are you, Adrian?" I mumble, staring out the window. If he's not back in half an hour, I'm going to find him myself.

The minutes tick down like an eternity, and, just as I'm about to grab the keys to the Jeep, a pair of headlights pull into the driveway. I sigh with relief. He's back.

CHAPTER FIVE
ADRIAN

It hadn't been easy losing the hunters. They must have found Serenity far earlier than we had, and they are determined to keep her. Thankfully, I'd taken an unassuming black car and changed the plates in the Lincoln Tunnel so they couldn't track us.

Serenity is tense beside me, clenching her purse to her chest tightly. I want to reassure her, but what can I say that won't just make her more frightened? I open my mouth what must be a thousand times, but there are no words to say.

"Where are we going?" she whispers as the

city disappears behind her. Behind us.

I glance over, and she's staring right at me. Looking into her blue eyes is almost painful, and I have to look away. "We have a cabin upstate. It's available for any of our people to use, and we've been staying there for a few weeks."

"We?" she looks even more worried all of a sudden.

I reach out to take her hand, then remember that she has no real reason to trust me. It doesn't matter that I can feel her aura, that my soul recognized hers the instant I first touched her. I pull away. "My men and I. We're a group of warriors whose job is to protect our kind from Hunters. We're also tasked with finding dragons that have been lost to us."

If she looked afraid before, she's now hard as stone, unreadable. How does she not believe that she could be a dragon? It had been obvious to me the moment I met her. There are few lost dragons left across the globe, but I'm the best tracker there is. In my search for Serenity, I've found dozens of lost dragons and returned them to our home.

"We're nearly there," I assure her. "You will have your own room until we can move you to a more secure location."

She barks out a single laugh, not for the first

time tonight. What could possibly be so funny about this situation? I bite back my words. She doesn't need me to intrude on her thoughts.

SERENITY

It's been an hour since we left the city, and I am no closer to knowing what's going on. Adrian said something about hunters, but I don't know why someone who likes to hunt would be a threat to me in my apartment. I hadn't questioned it, though, and I'd just gone with him. Now, in the car, that doesn't seem like the best move. Who just goes with a random stranger without telling anybody? On the rare occasion I take an Uber, I send Jenna a photo of the car, the driver, and the license plate before getting in.

I text my roommates that I won't be home tonight, and I Venmo my rent money to Jenna, as it seems I won't be seeing her tomorrow. My account reflects back a measly twenty dollars. Not even enough for groceries. How will I find a job in time to pay rent again next month?

Adrian had mentioned his men, and I can't help but wonder about them. There's basically no chance that their presence will be as immediately disarming as Adrian, but that's the least of my concerns. He may seem safe—I feel it in my soul, like we're connected or something—but what about these other men? Will they try anything funny with me? At least I'll have my own room. Hopefully with a lock or three.

We pull into a gravel driveway that's partially hidden by tall pines, and I take a deep breathe. I really hope I don't get murdered in a cabin in the woods. A shiver runs through me, and Adrian seems to mistake it for cold, as he turns the heat up.

"Thanks," I mumble, leaning as far from him as possible in the cramped car.

"Nobody will harm you here," he says, almost as if he's been reading my mind. Then again, he'd transformed into a monster earlier.

"Can you read my mind?" I ask. I can't help my curiosity.

A small smile creeps over his lips. "No, but I am able to sense your aura. I'm not sure how to reassure you, though. This situation is perhaps as strange to me as it is to you."

I snort. "Right. I'm sure."

He rolls his eyes, and I relax just a little. "Okay, probably not quite. But I'm not accustomed to bringing people home with me after a plain reconnaissance mission. There's usually quite a bit more vetting before the 'being whisked away' portion. I'm sure my men are in a panic right about now, as I was supposed to be home well over an hour ago."

"You didn't text them?" I ask, holding my phone up.

He suddenly looks concerned. "No. Too easy to trace. And I think you should turn your phone off just in case." Just like that, my small amount of ease with him is gone.

"I'd rather not," I say through my building panic.

He shakes his head. "Suit yourself. We will be somewhere they can't reach us by tomorrow afternoon, anyway."

I don't miss that he hasn't told me where this secret place is. Am I not supposed to know? I tap my fingers on my knee. I know what happens when someone is kidnapped and taken to a secondary location. Apparently, I have until tomorrow afternoon to escape. Maybe I can talk to Dad. Surely he'll make sure I don't end up homeless. Even if Mom hates me, he doesn't.

Through the trees, the golden light of a house begins to flicker. I expect us to pull into the driveway of a tiny hunting lodge, but, when we make it through the dense trees, there's a giant log cabin placed right in the center of a huge clearing. Nearly the entire front is made up of glass, and I spot the silhouette of a man standing at one window on the second floor.

"Who's that?" I ask, gesturing toward him just as he turns around and disappears through a door.

Adrian frowns. "That's Matthew. You'll meet him in a moment. As well as Dylan and Liam. They will have questions, but if you'd rather go to bed or shower or something, you don't have to socialize. I can deal with them."

I nod. The idea of being confronted by a group of military-types is pretty intimidating, especially after the day I've had. My phone rings again, and I silence it. Dad won't stop calling, so I text him that I'll call him back later. I won't plan my escape in front of Adrian.

"It will be alright," Adrian says, resting his hand on my shoulder. I should flinch away, recoil, but I lean into his touch, resting my head on his hand and closing my eyes. I'm so exhausted all of a sudden, and it seems silly, but it's almost like I can feel his heart speeding up at my actions.

He pulls the car to a stop.

"We should go in," he mumbles, but my eyes are so heavy that they're practically glued shut. "Serenity, are you awake?"

"Mhmm," I mumble. He sighs and gets out of the car, and I lean my head back on the headrest. Maybe I'll just rest my eyes for a few minutes before going inside. Suddenly, though, a blast of cold air comes at me from the right. Almost instantly, though, it's replaced by Adrian's warmth.

"I'm going to carry you inside," he whispers, lifting me almost effortlessly. I tuck my face into his chest, pulling his coat around myself to keep warm. When we fled my apartment earlier, I hadn't had time to grab my own coat. It's a miracle I'd even gotten my purse.

His heartbeat lulls me even more, and the voices from inside are distant when we enter.

"Where the hell have you been?" a pissed-off male voice demands. Adrian's arms tighten around me, and I burrow even further. The voice hisses. "And who the fuck is that?"

"Serenity," Adrian says, his voice wrapping around my name delicately. I perk up at the sound of my name, but I can't bring myself to open my eyes. "And she needs to sleep. I will discuss this with you when she's in bed."

The other voice doesn't argue, and Adrian

walks up some stairs. He opens a door and sets me in a bed, and I groan in protest as his body pulls away from mine. He sits on the bed beside me, covering me in what must be half a dozen blankets, then strokes my hair gently. When he hits a tangle, he expertly unties it to keep from harming me.

"Get some sleep, Princess. It's going to be a long day tomorrow," he whispers, leaning over me. His lips brush against my cheekbone as he speaks, and the skin heats up right there. I should be afraid of him, shouldn't trust him, but I want nothing more than for him to stay. And, if I wake up in the middle of the night, possibly more. No, I suppose it's best that he leaves. I will not be staying with these strange men, and I need to have my wits about me. "Goodnight."

With that, he's gone, and I drift off, dreaming of a tall man that rescued me. Of course, in my dreams, we're both wearing fewer clothes.

CHAPTER SIX
SERENITY

I awaken to bright light streaming in through the window, and I pull my blanket around me. As soon as I get up, I'll have to go back to work. Did someone open the door to my room overnight? It's usually pitch black in here.

Loud yelling from downstairs floats into my ears. *New York, am I right?* I chuckle to myself at the terrible joke, burrowing even further into my blankets.

Then, Adrian's voice penetrates my thoughts, and everything from last night comes flooding back. I'm not in my apartment, but a lonely cabin in the woods. I sit up and gasp, and my hands spark. I shake them out to get rid of the fire, but it's too late. The expensive-looking blankets on this huge bed are singed. *Well, at least they didn't catch fire*, my unhelpful brain reminds me.

I stand and hiss as my bare feet hit the hardwood floor. Did Adrian remove my shoes last night? I can't remember. I can't remember any of it. Everything after we arrived at the cabin is a blur, except the dirty dreams that are fresh in my mind. My shoes don't appear to be by the bed. Maybe Adrian put them by the front door? I still have to attempt to escape before they attempt to move me somewhere, in Adrian's words, more secure.

I wrap a fluffy sherpa blanket around myself and pad downstairs as quietly as possible.

"How can you even be sure it's her?" a man shouts. I try to place where I've seen him before, inspecting his lean-muscled body and long, messy brown hair. Right. He's the guy who'd been staring out the window last night. Matthew, my brain provides through the fog of the night.

"How can you not?" Adrian yells back, and I flinch. Adrian's back is turned to me, but when I startle, he turns around, and his anger turns to immediate concern. "Serenity. I'm sorry, I didn't mean to wake you."

I don't respond, just look between him and Matthew, who runs his hand through his beard. With his long hair and beard, not to mention the flannel shirt, he reminds me of either an actor or a lumberjack, though I can't decide which.

Someone else clomps down the stairs, and, before I can even process their presence, lifts me into a bridal carry.

"This must be the Princess," a jovial Irish voice says, far too loud and cheery for such a cold, early morning.

That's the second time someone has called me that. I have bigger problems than the strange pet name, though. "What the hell?" I squeal, thrashing my feet. Because of his grasp, though, my arms are trapped in the blanket.

Adrian's face hardens. "Dylan, put her down. Can't you tell that she's terrified?"

Dylan, who doesn't put me down, laughs, and it shakes my whole body. "Royalty shouldn't have to walk on cold floors," he says, taking me the rest of the way down the stairs and setting me onto the huge gray sectional, which I sink into. My heart races. *Who the hell are these people?* Now that he's standing in front of me, though, I can get a good look. He's leaner than the other two, and his pale blonde hair and clean-shaven face make him seem a lot younger. A wide grin is spread across his face, but there's something in his eyes I can't quite identify. A tension of some sort. "I'll get you some socks. You like pink?"

I frown. Did he just assume that because I'm a girl? Still, it's true. I really do like pink. I nod tersely, but he doesn't seem to notice my irritation. He goes over to a side table and opens the drawer, pulling out a pair of pink, faux-fur lined socks. I go to take them, but he sits at my feet and puts them on me himself. What the hell is with this guy? I can feel my face going red with embarrassment, but when I look at Adrian for help, his expression is filled with humor. I glance toward the front door, but my shoes aren't there, either.

"Serenity, this is Dylan. He's, ah, friendly." No shit, Sherlock. "Friendly but mostly harmless."

Well, that's reassuring at least. At that moment, though, Matthew turns on me, his face boiling with rage. "Dylan, we don't even know this girl. For all we know, she could be—" his voice turns from plain anger to straight disgust "—human."

Oh, fuck no.

I stand up, shucking the blanket, and Dylan actually lets me. I guess because of the socks. "Excuse you? And what is wrong with humans?"

I stomp toward him and jab my finger into his chest. "For all you know, it could be dragons that suck. Did you ever consider that?"

His eyes widen, and he spins on Adrian, totally blowing me off. "You told her?"

Adrian shrugs then walks past him to wrap me in his arms. Goosebumps rise on my arms, his heat enveloping me. And damn, I forgot how good he smelled. "Don't mind him," he mumbles. "He's a bit of an ass with new people. I promise he's not usually this bad." Adrian pauses, considering. "Actually, he is, but you get used to it."

I chuckle, putting my hands up against Adrian's chest.

"Oh for fuck's sake," Matthew says, his feet clomping on the ground as he storms off. I pull away from Adrian. I fell asleep so quickly last night that I didn't have time to formulate any sort of escape, but now, I can't help but wonder what these men plan on doing with me. Or to me.

"Is there a bathroom?" I ask shyly, batting my eyes at Adrian. Just as I thought he would, he smiles gently and nods, leading me to a hallway toward the back of the house.

"It's the last door on the right."

I nod, and I notice a back door to the house. Adrian may seem safe for me to be around, but

I can't trust anybody here. I almost died yesterday, and he just happened to show up to tell me
that I'm a dragon? I don't think so, and if they're
taking me somewhere else, somewhere presum-
ably far, then this is my only chance. I use the restroom quickly and then go to the back door. I
take one last look in the house, listening to Adrian and Dylan's muffled words from the front of
the house, and then run.

CHAPTER SEVEN
SERENITY

My only thought as I'm sprinting through the dense forest is, *I wish I'd learned to drive.* Then I could have just stolen one of their cars to get back to the city. The pounding at my apartment door had probably been a neighbor or something. The attack on me had been a random act of violence. I should call Dad, but fumbling at my pockets reveals that I don't have my phone on me. In my mind, I think of it sitting on the bed beside me. *Damn it, damn it, damn it.*

My socks become soaked quickly, and my toes are numb. I gasp for breath, and my lungs burn from the cold air. I have to stop and lean against one of the trees for a minute, but I can't risk being caught. What if they are truly dangerous? What if they hurt me? They'd seemed fine, but there's no way I can trust them. That's how you end up on Dateline. Adrian hadn't denied killing someone yesterday. If he's capable of that, then I have to assume he's capable of anything.

I run and run and run, but there's no sign of life anywhere. What if I'm just running in circles? After hours of this, I've gone from running to stumbling to straight-up shambling. I can no longer feel my feet, and my legs are numb.

Maybe if I just rest for a bit, I'll be better. There's hardly any snow on the ground here—the trees are too tightly bound together. I collapse on the ground at the base of a tree, curling in on myself in the leaves. This was a mistake. I'm hopelessly lost. Maybe if I'd just spoken to Adrian, he would've taken me home. He'd been nothing but kind to me. Instead, though, I'm going to die out here. Why didn't I at least bring a coat? My torn up coat at home isn't great, but it's better than freezing to death because I'm only wearing a light sweater.

As the sun filters golden through the trees, signaling the oncoming night, a huffing sound comes through the underbrush. I'm too cold to care, though. If a bear eats me, I probably won't even feel it. I'm basically a popsicle as it is.

Something bumps me, and I curl in on myself even more. The creature lets out a little noise, a sort of grumble that pierces through my shell of disinterest. I squeeze my eyes shut. Okay, I changed my mind. I don't want to get eaten by a bear. I stay as still as I can. Maybe it'll leave me alone if I just don't move. Greg said he saw a bear once, and the rule is to stay perfectly still until they lose interest.

I'm not prepared when, instead of a growl, I hear a gruff voice with the same strange accent as Adrian. "You must be Serenity. Nice to meet you." The man wraps me in a warm blanket that must have been heated and scoops me up into his arms, and I don't open my eyes. "It's not safe for you to be out here," he says. He keeps talking the whole walk back to the cabin, which takes hours. He doesn't complain, though, and he doesn't slow. Every time I come close to falling asleep, he gives me a little shake and asks a direct question. "What's your favorite movie?" he asks once.

I give a shaking answer that's barely more than a breath. "That new Mad Max movie."

He chuckles tensely. "Well, Furiosa wouldn't

freeze to death. And neither will you."

Another shudder runs through me, and I shove my face against his hot skin.

Finally the cabin appears in the distance, and I sigh with relief. The man holding me squeezes my body even tighter against him, a sigh coming from his throat as well. How worried could a stranger be? Even my own mom admitted that she doesn't care about my well-being. I clench the blanket tighter around me.

When the man walks us inside, Matthew's voice says, subdued, "Oh, thank god." Then, after a moment, "Guys, Liam found her. You can come back." He must be on the phone. Were they all searching for me? My heart warms at the thought, although I'm still not a hundred percent convinced they're not gonna murder me. Then again, I nearly died because of my own mistake, so I can't really say much about them when all they did was bring me here and wrap me in blankets and socks. At least if I get murdered here, I won't be cold. My thoughts take a detour as I taste the new name on my tongue. Liam. I don't say it aloud, but anyone looking at my face can probably tell what I'm thinking. He holds me tighter as Matthew says, "We need to get her warmed up."

"I know that, Matthew," Liam says, sounding

irritated. Oh, no. Are they going to fight like Matthew and Adrian had?

"I'm okay," I mumble, but it's not true. My feet are still numb, and probably purple. I don't dare open my eyes for fear of seeing my hands. I've spent so long suppressing the fire inside me that I had no idea how to call it up to me back in the woods. The one time I needed it, I couldn't have it.

Liam's arms tighten around me. "You will be."

He carries me across the house, Matthew walking ahead of us. There's a sudden rush of water, and Liam walks straight into the shower with me. I gasp at the sudden heat pounding my skin. Matthew's hands carefully work the frozen socks off my feet, and he sucks in a breath. "Shit. Shit shit shit."

That can't be good. When the water hits them, though, sharp pain ricochets up my body, and I cry out, digging my fingernails into Liam's skin as tears prick my eyes.

"It's alright," Liam says, his deep voice soothing. "You're going to be fine."

I open my eyes, only to finally realize that Liam is not wearing a shirt. Did he walk through the frozen woods with no shirt on? How is he not half-frozen as well? More importantly, how did I not notice that the entire time? Matthew is standing at my feet, covering them with his hands. His eyes are no longer angry, just frightened. Unlike Liam, he's fully dressed, and his long hair is stuck to his face and neck. He doesn't seem to notice or care, though.

"That bad?" I ask, and his head snaps up to me.

He gives me a pained smile. "Well, maybe don't go for a stroll in the snow when you're just wearing socks on your feet." I smile back as much as I can, but another shock of pain runs up my body. He frowns. "Sorry. It's gonna hurt for a bit. But I promise you're gonna be okay."

The back door opens.

"Serenity?" Adrian's voice calls, and my heart races. There's so much fear and pain in his voice that it makes me physically nauseous. I did that to him. I made him afraid. I barely know him, but I can feel the wrongness of his pain like it's a sucker punch to my own soul.

He runs into the bathroom—shirtless, for some reason. What is up with these guys?— and approaches me carefully. "Why would you do that?" he asks gentle, pressing his forehead against mine. I should mind this closeness, but it's like coming home. I breathe in his scent, letting the comfort wash over me. "I thought we'd lost you for good."

"I'm sorry," I whisper honestly. Maybe I should feel weird about being in a big walk-in shower with several near strangers, but I just feel cared for. For the first time in my life, I feel like I really, truly matter.

When Dylan arrives, he nods at me and goes out of the room, returning a few minutes later with steaming hot cocoa. "Drink this. It'll help."

Water from the shower head splashes into the cup, but I follow his instructions. He even holds it up to my lips for me, and Adrian kneads at my hands. A similar pain as my feet shoots up my arms, and I cough at a bit of the cocoa.

After a while, though, the pain subsides. When I can bear to look at them, my feet are bright red and a little tingly, like I sat on them for too long or something. Liam sets me on the floor of the shower, and everyone but Adrian leaves the room. The sound of the tension between us is deafening, but I'm not sure what to say to make him feel better. He's been nothing but good to me, and I ran away. I was the one leaving someone else behind this time. He turns around while I undress and wrap a fluffy robe around my body; then, he dries my hair out with a towel. The whole time,

I don't stand. I'm scared that I might not be able to if I tried.

"Please don't do something like that ever again," he says, voice strained. He stops toweling my hair and rests his forehead on the top of my head, and I sigh, half tempted to lean into his body and curl up in his arms.

"I won't," I promise. I turn around slowly and give in to the urge to press myself up against him, and he puts his arms around me. I trace my fingers over his hot skin, and he groans at the touch.

"You should go lie down," he says, voice strained. "We're wheels up in two hours."

I nod. "Will you stay with me?"

He sucks in a breath, then says, as quietly as possible, "Of course, Princess."

CHAPTER EIGHT
MATTHEW

I sit at the breakfast bar, resting my head in my hands. It's my fault she left. I know it is. I hadn't trusted Adrian's judgement, and it had almost gotten the girl killed. I still don't know for sure that she's a dragon—after all, what type of dragon almost freezes to death?—but she clearly matters to him on some deep level.

That's why I spent over an hour with her, making sure she wouldn't lose any appendages. Seeing the way Adrian looked at her the whole time had waves of guilt rolling through me, so much so that I could barely focus on healing her.

Adrian doesn't come back downstairs after taking her to bed. Of course he doesn't, though. She almost died trying to get away from us. Away from *me*. He won't leave her unattended for a moment until we're somewhere she can't run off and die. I'm certain of it.

"It's not your fault," Liam says, his presence sudden and surprising. "She was afraid of all of us. She second guessed trusting Adrian." I lift my head to look at him. "Reminds me of someone else."

I frown. Yeah, she is a lot like me. The only difference is that I've known Adrian for years and still didn't trust him about this. And I've trusted him with a lot more dangerous stuff than a possible dragon with no powers. "You really shouldn't read people's minds," I say.

He shrugs. "It's hard not to when their thoughts are so loud. Hers are especially strong."

I chew the inside of my cheek, considering the implications. Liam can only read the minds of other dragons, which means there's only one explanation. "So it's true," I say. "She is a dragon. Then why didn't she keep herself warm?"

He shakes his head and runs a hand through his short ginger hair. "I don't think she knows how. That's not uncommon with outsiders. If she wasn't raised by other dragons, then how would she know how to use her powers? It's not her fault."

I nod. That makes sense. But there's still one thing about her that bothers me. "Okay, but how do we know that she's this lost princess we're looking for? She was sent to live among humans when she was a baby."

Liam shrugs. "Adrian seems certain. That's plenty for me. After all, he is her fiancé."

CHAPTER NINE
SERENITY

A s it turns out, there is a private jet involved in the plan. Adrian stays with me every step of the way, even holding me in his lap on the car ride to the airport. When I expressed my concern for the lack of seatbelts, he'd said something about Liam's driving skills that had somehow convinced me. We have to wait for Dylan to get out of the middle row of seats to let us out, and Adrian passes me off to him like it's nothing while he gets himself out. I don't miss the way Adrian's eyes trace over my body the whole time Dylan holds me. Is that jealousy, or is it something else?

"I can walk, you know," I say, although I don't actually mind. The frigid winter chill sends a shiver through my body, and I can't help but recall the hours alone in the woods.

"No chance, Princess," Dylan says, holding me tighter before giving me back to Adrian.

"M'lords," the pilot says, saluting the guys as they climb aboard. "And m'lady," he says, his eyes crinkling at the corners as he kisses the back of my hand formally.

I flush, and Adrian straps me into one of the seats of a white leather couch when we board. Dylan brings me another hot cocoa, and I catch Matthew glancing at me every now and then. After everyone is boarded and the crew finishes their final check, Adrian straps in next to me and puts an arm over my shoulder.

"I've never flown before," I admit. "Actually, I've never left Manhattan before." This isn't something I've ever admitted, but it's true. My family never saw the need for extravagant vacations, instead choosing to spend school holidays in our townhouse in Midtown. On summer break, I had extra classes and tutoring to make up for my trouble in school.

"Well, it's not as scary as some people say,"

Adrian says. "I, for one, think you'd be an excellent flyer."

Right. He thinks I'm a dragon. I mean, I definitely believe that *he's* not human, and maybe the other guys, too, but I can't quite seem to make that leap about myself. My hands warm at the thought.

No, damn it. Magic hands aren't proof of being a dragon. I quell the supernatural heat inside of me before he can notice.

As the plane pulls toward the runway, I tense and grip Adrian's thigh with my right hand.

"It's alright," he says. "Thomas is the best pilot we have."

I close my eyes and breathe through my nose. The plane speeds up, and Adrian tightens his arm around me. I survived nearly freezing to death in a frozen forest, so I'll be pissed if I die in a plane crash.

The takeoff is smooth, though, and once we reach altitude, Adrian unhooks my seatbelt for me.

"I need to use the restroom," I admit. Adrian smiles, but there's that sadness tinged in his eyes.

"Don't try running off," he jokes. I smile back, but I don't reply. The pain in his tone is enough to make me want to curl into a ball and hide.

When I return, I sit in one of the armchairs across from Adrian. He looks a little hurt, but I can't focus when I'm sitting so close to him. I need to be logical in this situation. It's not like I've ever been whisked away by four handsome men with a private jet.

"Where are we going?" I ask. It feels like I've been asking that a lot lately.

"We're landing in Miami," Dylan says, moving over to the armchair next to mine. Somehow, he's had time to make a sandwich. "Then we'll be on the boat before morning."

"The boat?" I ask. Nobody told me anything about a boat. I picture a rinky little speedboat. How would we even fit on such a thing?

Liam is lying on another couch, his arm thrown over his face. "Draecus Island is a magical island with portals all over the world. The Pacific, the Antarctic, and I think they're putting one in the Baltic Sea soon. The nearest one to us is in the Caribbean, so we're going to sail there."

My stomach roils. The one time I've been on a boat was a horrible failure. Dad paid for a sailboat charter on the Hudson, and I spent the whole time vomiting in the boat's bathroom. Even if the boat is bigger than a speedboat, there's no way I will enjoy this leg of the journey.

"Don't worry, it's a Catamaran. And the weather is supposed to be nice, so it shouldn't be too rough."

I frown at Liam's words. "I don't know what that means."

Matthew walks in from the other room, crossing his arms over his chest. He doesn't look angry anymore, but his voice is still tense. What is his problem with me? "It's got two hulls, so it's a little more stable."

I nod, but I don't feel any better about this whole idea. Why can't we just fly to the island? I don't ask it aloud, though. Instead, I recline the armchair and turn on my side so I'm not looking at any of the guys. "I'm gonna try to get some sleep," I say.

The guys leave me alone, but I hear them mumbling to each other until I fall asleep. It seems that's all I've been doing the past couple days. Maybe I'll finally wake up to discover that this has all been a dream. A weird, sexy dream.

"Serenity, wake up," someone whispers, placing a hand on my shoulder. I crack my eyes open a sliver, but I'm not on the armchair anymore. Instead, I'm lying in a giant bed in a separate room of the plane. How did I get here?

I sit up and brush my hair out of my face. Adrian is sitting on the bed beside me, but he's wearing a different outfit. He's gone from a coat and tailored jeans to a plain gray t-shirt and pale blue swim trunks. It's a strange look for such a formal man, but it looks good.

"There are more clothes for you on the boat," he says when he notices me evaluating him. "We had one of our assistants pick up some appropriate attire."

I frown. "How do you know my size?"

"We checked when we dried your clothes earlier. I didn't think it would be proper for you to wear the same outfit for the whole trip. It's going to be a long week on the boat."

My frown deepens. "A week?" I couldn't handle a few hours on a boat as a teen, so a week will probably kill me.

"You'll be alright, Princess," he says, leaning closer to me. Close enough to kiss if I wanted. I breathe in his scent, but before we can get too close, I turn my head away. I can't get mixed up in something with Adrian. I don't even know him. Still, the pet name warms my heart. "Anyway," he says, leaning away from me and clearing his throat. "We'll be landing soon, so I thought you'd want to buckle up."

I nod and follow him back into the cabin, and as I stand, I realize that I'm wrapped not only in blankets, but in his coat. I press my face into the lapel and take a long sniff to inhale his woodsy scent. When I glance back up at him, he's turning his face back away from me, amusement written all over it. Heat rises in my neck and cheeks, and I smile shyly at him even though he's now looking away.

He lounges back on the couch, but he doesn't ask me to sit with him. Still, I move over to join him. His face instantly brightens, but I at least buckle myself in this time. I lay my head on his shoulder, and I catch Matthew looking at me once again. This time, I don't look away, challenging him. When the plane dips in altitude, he looks away and gathers his hair behind his head, tying it up in a ponytail. He runs a hand over his short, thick beard, the muscles in his arm flexing distractingly.

When the plane begins to circle for landing, the sun is just beginning to peek out over the ocean. The water glistens gold and teal, and the city sparkles below us. There are already people on the beaches, tanning and frolicking in the waves.

I lean even more into Adrian when the plane descends, and he rubs my back with one hand. Honestly, it's not that frightening, but I enjoy being in his arms. Maybe a week on a boat won't be so bad. Not if I'm with him, anyway.

I expect to be jolted when the wheels hit the airport tarmac, but it's smooth and easy. I only know we've landed because of the sound of the wheels screaming against asphalt.

After landing, everything moves in a rush. The air outside is hotter than I expected after the New York freeze, and I have to remove Adrian's coat so I don't break out in a sweat almost immediately. A driver puts the guys' bags in the trunk of a black SUV, and I sit in the backseat with Adrian. We drive through the streets downtown, then over a huge bridge. Finally, we pull into a harbor behind an upper-class real-estate development.

The heat is a shock to me as we unload the car in the parking lot of a marina, and I glance through the boats to search for the one they'd mentioned. All the ones parked where I can see seem really expensive, but none of the ones up close have two hulls like Matthew described. They're all just normal-looking sailboats. My stomach lurches at the mere thought of climbing aboard one of those things.

"This way," Dylan says enthusiastically, scooping me up into his arms again. I squeal but don't protest, and he carries me all the way down the lowest dock. Adrian's face stays cool and controlled when I look back at him, but once again, there's something off. I glance back out to the water, and that's when I spot it. I'd been expecting a little sailboat like the one we'd sailed in New York, like the ones at the docks, but the boat we're approaching is huge. It's longer than any of the others, so long it can't be parked in one of the marina spots. Instead, it's anchored further out in the harbor, long and black and sleek.

"What is that?" I ask, incredulous. It must be nearly a hundred feet long. Dylan laughs and sets me on the dock.

"That's the boat," he says, and I roll my eyes. He laughs again, so the expression on my face must be ridiculous. "It's a Sunreef 80. I think the palace bought it last year."

I frown. Even from here, I can tell that this thing must have cost a million dollars.

Liam leans over me and whispers, "Ten million."

I startle and look at him. "Did you just read my mind?"

He nods, looking completely serious.

My mouth pops open in a little O. Adrian said he could read auras, but I didn't expect anyone to actually be able to read *minds*. The realization that he might have heard any of my impure thoughts about Adrian sends a flood of heat through my face.

"Alright, everyone. Into the dinghy," Matthew says, his usual grouchy self. I reach up and tug gently on his ponytail, and he grimaces. "Rude." Still, I can see the tiniest twinkle of amusement in his generally stoic face. I smirk at my little victory over him.

He takes my hand and helps me climb into the little inflated rubber boat. My skin warms against his, and he gives me the barest smile.

Well, well, well. The man has feelings after all.

Everyone piles into the dinghy, and Liam steers us toward the colossal boat. As we approach, I read the word Firefly on the back. That must be the registered name of the vessel. When we arrive, he pulls the dinghy onto a platform at the back, and we all climb off. The boat doesn't even rock a little with our movement, and I follow the guys up the steps from the lower part of the boat, and the main deck leaves me in awe.

The floor is a pale wood, and there are black marble tables with white-cushioned booths with modern glass lamps hanging above them. To one side is a black floating staircase made of that same wood, which goes up to yet another deck. The humid Florida air is sticky and oppressive, so I go through the paned glass doors into a lounge and kitchen area. There's even air conditioning blasting at me from the vents. This area is just as grand, custom lighting hanging from the ceiling to bring an intimate feeling to the three—*three!*— sets of tables across the room.

"This is ridiculous," I say incredulously, sitting on one of the two giant gray sectionals—the one with two coffee tables instead of a giant marble dining table.

Dylan shrugs and sits next to me, propping his feet up on the coffee table. His heat radiates off of him, but he isn't touching me. His eyes flicker up to Adrian, but the humor never leaves his face. "You get used to it."

I roll my eyes. I seriously doubt I could get used to a ten million dollar yacht. My parents are well-off, but they aren't *borrow a fancy boat whenever they want to* rich. At least, if they were, they wouldn't tell me about it.

"Serenity," Adrian says, and I turn to look at him, resting my head on the couch, "would it be alright with you if I went grocery shopping?"

I consider this question for a minute. Will I be okay staying on this boat without Adrian? Even for just a little while? I haven't spent much time with the other men. In fact, Liam is the only other one I've been alone with, and I was half a popsicle at the time. I nod. "Yeah, I'm good."

He looks over the other guys, and they exchange a significant glance before he turns and walks off the boat. So now I'm alone with the other three.

"Wanna watch a movie?" Dylan asks, clicking a button on a remote. A TV screen outside unfolds from the ceiling, and Dylan hops right back out of the seat, holding a hand out for me.

I don't really want to leave the comfortable AC, but his charm is irresistible. "Sure," I say, taking his hand. He bows down and kisses the back of mine, and I blush and pull myself up while Matthew watches us. "You guys are really odd," I say.

"Princess, you have no idea."

CHAPTER TEN
SERENITY

Apparently, living on a boat is hard. First thing the next morning, we leave Miami, the boat rocking gently over the waves. Soon enough, I'm curled up in my private cabin, a room that's somehow larger than my bedroom in New York despite the fact that it's on a boat. My stomach lurches with every new wave, and Dylan quickly gave up trying to get me on deck to watch the sea. "Maybe tomorrow," I'd lied. At this rate, I will be in this room either until we dock or until I die, whichever comes first.

Probably death.

As the boat hits a particularly harsh wave, I leap out of bed and stumble to the toilet so I can throw up. At least I'm alone so that nobody else can see how awful this is for me. Still, I can't imagine being able to put up with this for the full week of travel.

A quiet knock sounds at the frame, and I groan, resting my forehead on the toilet seat. "Adrian, please go away," I mumble.

Footsteps approach me, and he crouches down after flushing the toilet. "Actually, Adrian told me to come check on you."

Fantastic. I am not ready to deal with *him*.

"Matthew, no offense, but I'm having a bad enough day without being around someone who hates me," I say. I turn my head, and the smallest bit of hurt crosses his usually stoic eyes.

"I don't hate you," he says, putting the back of his hand against my forehead.

I roll my eyes and lean away. Since the vomiting is over for now, I'd rather not have my face up against a toilet. "Sure you don't." He hasn't spoken to me since we boarded the boat last night, and now I'm not really sure what to do with his confession. Could it be true that he doesn't hate me?

"I really don't," he replies earnestly. "I was being an ass when we first met, and I'm sorry about that. But I came down here to help you."

As the boat comes crashing on yet another wave, my stomach heaves. Matthew immediately gathers my hair in his hand while I puke into the toilet bowl some more. This situation could not possibly be less dignified. He rubs his other hand on my arm, and goosebumps rise on my flesh. I want to pull away, but the motion is soothing, and it's almost like my nausea sinks away through the tiled bathroom floor.

"Better?" Matthew asks, and I close my eyes and nod. It doesn't make sense that what basically amounted to a pat on the arm made me feel so much better. "I have healing powers. Kind of like Adrian being able to sense auras and Liam being able to read minds."

Of course he can. That's why he'd been at my feet after Liam found me in the snow. I hadn't seen the extent of the damage, but I probably should have lost a toe or two. Instead, I'm totally back to normal. "What can Dylan do?" I ask. When the boat hits a wave again, my body doesn't react. Still, the motion throws me off balance, and I crash into Matthew.

"That's not for me to say," he says quietly, his cheek pressed against mine and his arms wrapped around me. My heart speeds up, but I don't pull away. Matthew may be prickly, but somewhere deep down, he cares.

After a moment of sitting with him, I push off his chest gently. His eyes are dark and stormy, and I know I could drown in them if I'm not too careful. I don't remove my hands from his chest, and my breath catches in my throat when his eyes flick to my lips.

A knock startles us both, and we practically leap away from each other. I sway with the movement of the boat, but it doesn't make me sick again. Thank goodness for little miracles. My eyes trace over Matthew once again. Well, thank goodness for *him*.

"Guys, there are dolphins!" Dylan exclaims from the other side of the door. My eyes widen, and I look back at Matthew. His intense, evaluating look is gone, replaced by that same wall that he's always kept between us. Is he always like this, or is it just with me? Now that I've seen past his flat exterior, though, I want more of it. So much more.

I reach out to him, and, carefully, like he's unsure of himself, he takes my hand.

"I don't want to get sick again," I explain. When we exit the room, Dylan notices our intertwined hands, and his eyes glisten with something that I can't identify. Something almost sad. Then, I lead Matthew upstairs and onto the bow of the boat, where there are big pieces of thick woven fabric attached between the two hulls. *Trampolines*, Adrian had called them, although they aren't bouncy at all.

Sure enough, there are dolphins weaving below our boat, jumping in and out of the surf. Their slick bodies are almost close enough to touch. My heart soars, and Matthew has to wrap an arm around my waist to keep me from leaning too far and flying overboard. I glance back at him with a grin, and he's holding on to the steel cable that goes from the bow of the boat all the way up to the top of the mast. When he catches me looking at him, he smiles just a little, although his eyes remain distant. Another victory for me, no matter how small. I tuck myself into him, my back pressed up against his hard chest. I half expect him to push me away, but he adjusts his arm to hold me tighter.

If Matthew hadn't come down to help me, I'd be missing out on the most gorgeous teal ocean I've ever seen. It shouldn't be possible for anything real to be this bright blue-green, yet here it is, right in front of my eyes. I wrap one of my

hands just above Matthew's around the steel cable and take in a deep breath. In New York, every
moment felt like the lead-up to something bad.
Overdue rent, getting fired, being practically dis-
owned. Now, though, I'm standing with a beautiful man that I'm just beginning to understand,
and the air tastes like hope.

I don't pay too much attention to where the boat
is going, but, just as the sun begins to sink,
we reach an island that looks abandoned. Small
waves crash upon the distant white shore. I sit in
one of the booths upstairs, wrapped in a blanket
while the guys get to work collapsing the sails.
When we get closer to the island, Matthew drops
the anchor, and I lean over the rail and smile at
him. He catches my eye, and it almost seems like
he blushes. That can't be right, though. It must
just be the sun on his cheeks.

I take another deep breath, and someone comes
up the stairs to the deck where I'm lounging. I
turn lazily to find Liam carrying a giant serving
dish with tons of food on it. Has he been cooking
while the other three sail? He sets it down on the
table and takes the spot in the booth right next to

me without a word.

"The others will be just a few minutes," he says, doling out portions of meat and vegetables and a rich brown sauce that makes my mouth water.

I take a bite and groan. This is the best thing I've ever eaten. Over the past couple of days, I've mainly been snacking for sustenance, and this morning I'd been too ill to eat. Now, though, the home-cooked food is a blessing. Almost enough for me to consider dragging Liam into bed.

"Tell me about dragons," I say through bites of food.

Liam pricks an eyebrow. "What would you like to know?"

I would like to ask how I'm supposed to choose just one of the guys. I mean, Adrian is the one who saved me in New York, the one who's been at my side almost constantly, the one who comes to me when I need him. Still, I can't help but feel drawn to the rest of them. Matthew with his prickly exterior and secretly soft heart, Dylan with his contagious optimism, and Liam with his stoic face but caring nature. Instead, I ask, "I don't know. Politics and stuff?"

Liam frowns and stares at me for so long that heat crawls up my face. Right. He can read minds. "Dragon culture is different from most human cultures," he says slowly, keeping eye contact with me. "There are far fewer women than there are men, so it's very common for households to contain one woman and several husbands."

My heart stops. Multiple husbands? I know that polyamory is a thing, but it's not something I'd ever actually considered for myself. It's still so taboo in the human world, although it has always sounded so appealing when I've heard about it. For me, it's been easier to just avoid getting tied down. That way, nobody gets hurt. I swallow a lump that's forming in my throat, but my eyes are stuck on Liam's. "Oh," I whisper.

"You, Princess, could have anyone you want," he continues, his eyes flickering to my lips for just an instant. I lean toward him. Is it true? Could I have anyone? Or, at least, the ones I want to have?

As I'm about to ask, Dylan comes clomping up the stairs. I jerk away from Liam, who I'm very nearly touching. He looks amused. Had it all been a joke? I look down at my plate, and a lump forms in my throat and tears prick at my eyes. Of course he would tease me with that. It's too good to be true.

A hand slides onto my thigh, and Liam's breathe tickles my ear. "It wasn't a joke, Princess. You just looked so embarrassed. There's no need for that here. Not with us." Then, like there's nothing wrong with it, he presses his lips to my temple. Dylan rolls his eyes, but something dark flickers in his expression once again.

"What's wrong?" I ask, and he looks surprised. I haven't spoken to Dylan much, but his presence is comforting. He's never seemed upset with me, and I don't want that to start now.

He smiles, but it's pained. "Nothing. I'm just tired."

He's lying for some reason, but I can't figure out what it is. Maybe I should try talking to him alone.

When Adrian appears on deck with Matthew not far behind, they pause at the sight of me pressed up against Liam's side. Adrian looks from me to Liam, then comes around and joins on my other side.

"How are you feeling, Princess?" he whispers in my ear. With Liam's hand on my thigh, this intimate moment feels forbidden. I can't be certain that Liam had been telling the truth, but Adrian doesn't seem to mind the closeness.

"Why do you all keep calling me that?" I ask. Adrian pulls away, his face strange. Is he upset with me?

Matthew looks between us, then stands up,

bracing his hands on the tabletop. "You didn't tell her?" he asks, anger concealed through layers of self-control.

"I was going to wait until the appropriate time," Adrian says, immediately defensive. He pulls away from me, and I almost protest, but Liam puts an arm around my shoulders and holds me close.

"It would be best if you stayed back," he whispers, and a shiver runs down my spine. What does that mean? I could see Matthew being dangerous, but Adrian? I reach a hand out and brush it down his arm and over his hand, and he spins to look at me. His eyes are crazed, like a wild animal that's been trapped. They're that unnatural golden color once again. I jerk away, and his eyes turn hurt. Before I can say anything, though, he sprints to the edge of the deck and leaps off.

I cry out, reaching my hand toward him like I can keep him from crashing down to the deck below or diving into the water, but there's nothing I can do. Instead of getting hurt, though, his body shifts and cracks until he's not Adrian anymore, but a huge brass dragon, like something out of a fairy tale.

I'd seen his features turn monstrous in my apartment, but, until now, I'm not sure I believed that these men were actual dragons. He's at least as large as the boat, and his body is covered in glistening bronze scales that catch the sunset. Ivory horns spiral atop his massive head, and a burst of air tosses my hair in my face when he beats his massive wings. Before I can do anything else, though, he disappears past the island. Matthew follows behind, transforming just like Adrian had.

I should run, get somewhere safe, but there's nowhere to go. We're at a random island somewhere south of Miami with nobody else in sight. Instead, I force my way out of Liam's arms and run all the way down, back to my cabin. There's no way this tiny room on a flimsy boat could be safe from a *freaking dragon attack*, but it's not like I have any other options.

CHAPTER ELEVEN
LIAM

Serenity is gone. She'd been disgusted and terrified when Adrian and Matthew transformed. Of course she had, though. Adrian, the one who she trusts most, never actually told her about her heritage. Then, he transformed right in front of her with zero warning. I pace the main deck, then walk out to the bow, then go for a swim in the inky black water, then pace some more. I can't speak with Serenity. She may have locked herself downstairs, but her thoughts are so loud that she could be standing next to me.

She wants out, and she's terrified of all of us.

Of me.

As soon as Adrian returns, I'm going to punch him in the face.

Matthew, too, if it doesn't make me feel better.

Eventually, though, I get bored of pacing. I go to the back of the boat and take the few steps down the very rear where the water laps at the hull, sitting and dipping my feet in the cool water. I rest back on my elbows and watch the night sky, stars twinkling above as longing builds up inside me.

It wasn't supposed to be like this. Female dragons may take multiple mates, but Adrian is Serenity's fiancé. They were chosen for each other at birth, bound by magic to find each other no matter what. So why is it that I can't stop thinking about her? Or that she seems to gravitate toward me? Why was I the one who found her in the woods when Adrian was the one who found her in the city?

I close my eyes and let the cool sea breeze wash over me. If I get too worked up, I'm going to transform, and it's pretty clear how Serenity feels about that. I don't want to frighten her like the others had.

Someone walks toward me on the deck, his thoughts loud and clear.

How is she?

"Not great, Adrian. But I'm sure you knew that already," I say through gritted teeth.

He sighs, and, out loud, he says, "I'm sorry. I know I should have told her. But..." I wait, not even bothering to look at him. "But every time I tried, I remembered how terrified she was when I shifted even a little bit in her apartment. You weren't there, so you didn't see it. It was like..."

I frown. I know where he's going with this. "Like you were a monster?"

He sits on the steps above mine. I really should punch him, but instead of being angry, I'm just tired. "We'll discuss it with her in the morning. She needs to know about herself. Her birthright. She can already sense it. She has powers she doesn't understand, and a connection with you that she can't deny. For now, though, we should just let her sleep." I don't mention the connection I feel with her. There's so much going on, and it isn't pertinent.

Adrian's thoughts rise up in protest, but he just says, "Alright."

I don't sleep. Instead, I putter around the boat, cleaning parts and tightening lines and adjusting instruments. By the time morning comes around, the sea is still as glass, and a cloudy sky has opened up for rain to spill out over us. Off in the distance, a flock of birds gathers as the water churns with fish below. Every few seconds, I spot the fins of dolphins in the swarm.

"I never knew the rain could be so beautiful," Serenity says, and I jump. How did she sneak up on me? Nobody ever sneaks up on me. It's too difficult when I can hear their thoughts from a mile away.

"Yes," I agree, but I don't look at her. I will not scare her off like Adrian and Matthew had last night. I pretend to be working, taking a line from its hook and re-winding it even though it's perfect from my work overnight.

"What aren't you guys telling me?" she asks, even closer than before. Close enough to touch? I shove the thought away. Still, her flowery scent washes over me, and the tension in my shoulders releases.

I shrug. "It's something Adrian should tell you, I think." I re-do the line for the third time. I don't want to give her a reason to leave, but when her forehead presses against my spine, I freeze.

"Please," she says. She doesn't sound scared or angry, just tired. I know the feeling. "I need to know."

Slowly, to avoid spooking her, I turn. She's wearing different clothes than yesterday, a pair of burgundy shorts with a high-neck bikini top that has a green plant print. She has so much skin showing, and I want nothing more than to trace my hands over her and memorize every piece of her body.

My mind is in turmoil, so it takes me a few seconds to remember that I'm supposed to answer her question. "Twenty-seven years ago," I say, taking her hand in mine as carefully as I can, "there was a war in Draecus. Some citizens believed that humans were below us, and they believed that dragons should rule over humanity."

"Dragons like Matthew?" she asks.

I shake my head. "I don't agree with all of Matthew's ideals, but, deep down, he is a good person. There's a lot he doesn't understand about humans, and a lot of his beliefs stem from his father. The dragons I'm talking about..." I consider my words carefully for a long time. I don't want to scare her off. My thumb traces over hers, and, although I'm not sure she realizes it, her body is leaning toward mine. "They had ideas that they were going to act upon. They didn't believe that human-born dragons were real dragons, or that half-blooded dragons deserved the same rights as the rest of us."

Serenity's thoughts are racing, but I do my best to keep from invading her privacy. I continue, "At the height of the war, your parents decided to send you away. To hide you in the human world. They didn't believe in the rebels' ideals, and they feared that you would come to harm if you stayed on the island." At this, her eyes widen marginally. Her questions stall in her head, all of them about her parents. I reach a hand up to her cheek, and she leans into my touch. Her skin is cold, and I wish I could wrap her in my arms to keep her warm. To keep her safe.

"With the war, though, came the return of dragon hunters. Some of the rebels got cocky, and dragon hunters destroyed them. A treaty was signed between the rebel groups and the royal family, and it was decided that you would be brought back to Draecus Island. Warrior groups were sent all over the world to search for you, monitoring strange activity and Hunter groups."

"Why me, though?" she asks. "Why do I matter?"

I close my eyes. This isn't my story to tell. Adrian is the one who's connected to her, the one who is supposed to care for her. Still, with Serenity so close, I can't help myself. She needs to know, and Adrian is fast asleep in his own cabin.

"Your mother is the Queen of Draecus Island," I say. "You are the only heir to the throne, and possibly the only hope for the survival of Dragonkind."

She gasps and pulls away from me, but our fingers are still intertwined. I watch her for signs of distress, any sign that she's going to run away from me.

"I can't be," she whispers. "I'm just some girl. I'm not smart or regal or anything. I can't be a...a...."

I frown and supply the word, "Princess?"

Before she can respond, Adrian interrupts. "Serenity, I should have told you."

She drops my hand and turns to him. The loss of her touch is like a stab through the heart, but it's not me she's bound to. She goes to him, and I go to bed.

CHAPTER TWELVE
SERENITY

Adrian and I go to the bow of the boat, sitting across from each other on one of the two trampolines. I trace the weave of the white fabric instead of making eye contact with him.

"Is it true?" I ask, looking up at him through my eyelashes. Water soaks through my hair, plastering it to my skin. He nods, his eyes so sad that it could kill me, but I don't move closer.

"There's more," he says. His voice is strangled, like whatever he has to say is going to ruin his life. I wait, and, after he considers his words for a few minutes, he goes on. "When you were born, it was agreed that you would be engaged to the son of a human-born. A dragon born from human parents. Your mother used a spell to bind you, to ensure the two of you were connected. That you'd always find each other." He chews his lip.

In my heart, I know he's talking about himself. I scoot toward him and lay my hand on his. "You're human-born?" I ask. Right now, I want nothing more than to take his pain away.

He nods. "My parents came to the island when I was little. To protect me from rebels that wanted me dead. That was when your mother bound us together. I was only five, but I remember the ceremony like it was yesterday. After you were sent away, I couldn't function. I couldn't eat, couldn't sleep. I went into the military as soon as I could. When your mother decided it was time to find you, I volunteered. It took me years of searching, but..."

I squeeze his hand, and he leans toward me and rests his forehead on my shoulder. "I'm so sorry," he whispers, his voice raspy. "I should have told you. I should have said it immediately. I was a coward."

I consider this revelation. That we're bound together. I don't ask why he didn't find me immediately, though. I just wrap my arms around him and hold him, and we sit in the rain for what feels like hours.

When the downpour lets up, I say gently, "We should probably go get changed."

He nods, standing up and going to walk away from me, but I latch onto his arm like I can't be without him. There's definitely a connection between us, but I'm not sure what it means. If there's this connection, then why do I feel so much longing for the others, too?

Still, I walk downstairs with Adrian. His cabin is in the same hall as mine, and I'd heard him pacing by my door last night when he returned. I let him go into his room, and, before I'm finished changing into a pale pink one-piece swimsuit, he knocks gently at my door.

I finish tying a gray sarong around my waist and open the door. His eyes move down my body for a moment before returning to my face, and he clears his throat. "I was thinking that we might not leave quite yet," he says. I raise an eyebrow, and he continues, "I think we could all use a day to unwind."

I consider this, then nod. "That sounds nice." Suddenly, a burst of sunlight shines into my bedroom. "I guess the rain is done."

Instead of going outside to sun on the deck,

though, I intertwine my fingers with Adrian's and pull him close. He's wearing a pair of black swim trunks and a gray t-shirt, and I lay my spare hand on his chest to feel his heart pounding. Water laps gently at the hull, and I stand up on my tip-toes to press my lips against his jaw.

He swallows, and when I pull away, his eyes are closed. "Serenity, you don't have to do this," he says. "You and I may have been bound by a spell, but it's still your life. You can do anything you want. Whether you want to be with me, or Liam, or Matthew…"

I pull away, and Adrian looks at me, a sad smile on his face.

"Is what Liam said true?" I ask. My heart is racing, and my hands shake.

Adrian shakes his head, not in disagreement, but like he's clearing it.

"Which part?"

I swallow. This is probably the worst thing I've ever had to ask anybody. My face burns, and I have to look away from him to force the words out. "About women having more than one…" I can't even finish the sentence, and the question makes me nauseated.

Adrian tucks a finger below my chin and guides my face up to look at him. "Is that something you'd want?" At this moment, his face is unreadable. I have no idea what he's thinking. Did my question offend him? Still, I choose honesty and nod.

He smiles. "It's true," he says. "In fact, it's pretty much expected. And I would be honored to belong to you."

I don't give it a second thought. I lean up on my tip-toes and throw my arms around his neck, dragging him down for a kiss. He reciprocates instantly, wrapping his arms around my waist and lifting me up, carrying me to the bed. He sets me down, and I lean on the mountain of pillows.

He doesn't come to me immediately, instead kissing gently up my leg, from my foot all the way up to my hip bone. His lips are like fire trailing up me, and I have to grit my teeth to keep from moaning at his touch. He keeps going, kissing me on my belly, then my sternum, then my collar. He goes achingly slow, and I dig my fingers into his hair and drag his face to mine, his five o'clock shadow rough against my skin as our lips dance desperately.

"You have no idea how long I've wanted this," he whispers, and I move my hands down and grasp at the hem of his shirt. He understands immediately and sits up, straddling me and pulling his shirt up over his head. I rest my hands on his lower stomach, the hard muscles and his heaving breaths causing me to clench my thighs together. I want to touch him, want to feel him against me. Inside me. I sit up, but at this angle, his face is far too high for my lips to reach, so I kiss his chest and savor our bodies pressed together.

When someone knocks on the door, though, I groan in frustration.

"There's lunch in the galley," Dylan calls, then his footsteps trail away. I groan and lean back, and Adrian lies back over me, pressing his forehead against mine.

"We should probably go," he says, his breath tickling my lips. I nod, and, instead of helping me stand, he lifts me off the bed and carries me upstairs.

Liam's eyes are on fire as he watches us enter, but Adrian sets me down next to him on the couch. Is it that obvious that I have feelings for Liam, too? I catch them giving each other a meaningful look, and then Liam nods, his face brightening by about a million degrees. Adrian must have told him with his thoughts, and I can feel myself blushing for the thousandth time.

Liam makes me a plate and puts a hand on my thigh. His touch is electric, and a thrill runs through me as Adrian takes the hand on my other side. Matthew watches this whole exchange with curiosity, but, as usual, his face is unreadable. Curiosity flickers in Dylan's eyes, but he doesn't say anything throughout the meal. This whole situation is so surprising and confusing that I hardly eat, although Liam's chicken fajitas are the best I've ever had.

"I was thinking we might go for a swim," Dylan says, cutting through the silence.

Matthew shrugs. "I'm not really in the mood."

The other two agree, seemingly considering my face. At that moment, I make a decision. Maybe this will be a good chance for me to learn about the fourth dragon on this boat. "I'd love to go for a swim," I say. If I'm in paradise on a ten million dollar boat, I might as well test the waters, too.

DYLAN

Serenity is stunning in her pale pink swimsuit that I picked out. Of course, I'd never tell her that I picked it, but the fact that she's wearing it sends warmth bursting through me. We take the dinghy away from the boat, beaching it on the island. She clings to one of the hand-holds as we crash over the breaking waves, and she lights up when her toes squish into the snow-white sand.

"This place is amazing," she says, stretching her hands out above her. I just watch, but then, a mischievous idea pops into my head. I stride toward her quickly, then pick her up and put her over my shoulder. Her skin is softer than anything I've ever touched, and she screams and laughs as I carry her toward the surf.

"Put me down!" she demands through a laugh. I'm tempted to turn my head and kiss the thigh that's up against my cheek, but she's not mine for the taking. It's pretty clear that she wants Liam and Adrian, and possibly even Matthew, but she hasn't shown any interest in me. *Not that it matters*, my brain reminds me.

"As you wish," I say when the water gets up to my chest. Then, I let her go and plummet into the water. When I come back up, she's sputtering and giggling, and I can't help but notice a specific drop of water trailing down her collar and into her cleavage. I shut down that thought as quickly as I can. If she just wants us to be friends, I'll have to be okay with that.

"That wasn't nice," she says, slapping me playfully on the arm. I grin, watching her watch me.

It's hard to gauge exactly how she feels about this whole situation, especially because I can't sense her aura or read her mind. It must be so much easier to be Adrian or Liam.

I brush her long hair out of her face. "Maybe I'm not a nice person."

She frowns. "Of course you are. You might be the nicest person I've ever met."

Her words bring my heart to a gallop. She wouldn't say that if she knew anything about me. She's only known me for a few days, and she only sees what I allow her to see. I can't help but recall yesterday, though, when she'd asked me what was wrong. She'd been paying close enough attention to notice my discomfort, although I hadn't been willing to admit what was bothering me.

She tilts her head, her eyebrows scrunching together. "Are you alright?"

Crap. I've been standing here too long, and now she's getting suspicious.

"Just planning a bunch of crimes," I joke. "Mean crimes. Like kicking puppies."

She laughs and puts her hands over her mouth. "Wow. Maybe you aren't a nice person."

I know she's joking, but I also know that she's right. Matthew may be standoffish and prickly,

but he's a good person at heart. If she knew anything about me, she'd run away screaming. I roll
my eyes, but she still has that look of concern in
her eyes. To avoid talking about it, I lift her into a
bridal carry and toss her into the waves.

After a few hours of playing in the water and
sunning on the beach, I wrap Serenity in a
towel and drive her back to the Firefly. She sits
beside me and lays her head on my shoulder, and
I push away the distracting thoughts in my head.
When we arrive at the boat, I help her out of the
dinghy.

Dinner is ready in the galley, and she sits next
to me, Adrian on her other side. Always Adrian.
He gives me a look of warning, and I nod. He
knows exactly what I'm capable of, and he just
needs to know that I'm not going to hurt her. He
was probably keeping an eye on Serenity's aura
the whole time we were at the beach just to be
sure.

"This is delicious, Liam," she says through a
mouthful of spaghetti. His face brightens marginally at her words. Now that she knows how
dragon households work, she seems more com-

fortable around everybody. Still, she shouldn't see me the same way as the others.

"Thank you," Liam replies. "I made everything from scratch."

"You'll have to teach me how to do that," she says, slurping up more noodles. Liam's eyes darken, and he smiles.

"I'd rather you never have to cook again. I like cooking for you."

My heart twinges. I will never have something like they have. That connection. I don't deserve it, but it still hurts to see it happening right in front of me. I smile through the pain, though, as I've always done. I will be better than I was. And then, sometime far in the future, I might be worthy of the type of affection Serenity gives out freely.

CHAPTER THIRTEEN
SERENITY

We sail out first thing the next morning. I spend a lot of time at the helm with Adrian, and he explains the different instruments to me. Matthew pretends to be bothered by my presence when we adjust the sails, but I catch him smiling more than once throughout the journey. Liam seems glad to teach me about the different lines, but when I join him in the kitchen, he refuses to teach me to cook.

"A princess should never have to cook her own meals," he says, sprinkling some sort of seasoning on a piece of fish that he'd filleted earlier today.

The boat doesn't stop for days. I expect us to stay at islands throughout the journey, perhaps take a break, but the boat is constantly moving. Instead of inviting any of the guys into my room, I sleep alone.

On the third night of this, a jolt wakes me, and I stand and wrap myself in a blanket, staying barefoot as I pad up to the helm. All is quiet but the sea rushing by us, and I squint to try to see anything on the horizon, but it's all just darkness. It's like we're our own little floating bubble.

Dylan is at the helm, his short blonde hair hidden under a hooded sweatshirt.

"Evening," I say, leaning back on the low wall on his other side.

He turns his head to me and smiles. "Does Adrian know you're up here?" he asks.

I stiffen. "Adrian doesn't need to know my whereabouts at all times." Do I spend too much time with Adrian, then? I haven't meant to, but I guess I do tend to gravitate toward him. And if we were bound together when I was born, then it makes sense.

He shrugs. "I just don't want any trouble is all. Adrian can be a bit defensive when it comes to me."

I tilt my head. Why would Adrian be defensive toward Dylan? Dylan, who's been nothing but kind to me since we met. "I doubt you get into more trouble than me," I say. After all, the guys have had to save me from dying twice.

He doesn't meet my gaze, but his lips twist into a frown. "You have no idea." I watch his face for any change, a break in his stoic expression that shows he's playing some sort of joke on me, but it doesn't come. I look out into the moonless night, the sea spray sending a shiver down my body. "Are you cold?" he asks, but he still doesn't look directly at me, just tilts his head in my direction.

I bite my lip and nod.

"You should go back inside, then," he says.

I shake my head and look at my bare feet. "I don't know why you're being like this," I say, "but it's not like you."

That seems to get him. He turns his eyes directly on me, holding me down with his heavy gaze. "You don't know anything about me."

At that moment, the boat hits another wave, and I stumble. As if working on instinct, he reaches out and grabs me, pulling me right up against his chest. I take in a breath, and he smells like salt and earth and something else I can't identify. Something sweet.

When he realizes what he's done, Dylan lets me go, but I cling to him.

"You can't do this. You need to leave me alone," he says matter-of-factly.

I shake my head. "I don't think that's what you want. And it's definitely not what I want."

He stiffens for a moment, then buries his face in my hair, a deep shuddering breath running through him. Slowly, carefully, his arms wrap around me. We stand together for what could be a lifetime, but it's not enough when we're interrupted.

"Serenity," a voice says from the doorway to the galley. I turn my head, and Matthew is standing there, his eyes wide and his knuckles white against the door frame. His hair is a mess, the ponytail barely holding itself together.

I hold on tighter to Dylan, but he releases me from his grasp.

"What's going on?" I ask. My heart speeds up. "Is everyone else alright?"

Matthews eyes dart from me to Dylan and then back to me. Then, he holds out his hand. "Serenity, come inside with me."

My throat closes up, and my breath stops. Something serious must be going on for Matthew to be acting this way. I step away from Dylan, then place my hand delicately in Matthew's. Immediately, he tightens his grip and pulls me up against him. What the hell is going on? He drags me into the galley and lifts me into a bridal carry.

"What is it?" I ask, my heart practically pounding its way out of my chest. "Is someone hurt?"

He takes me downstairs and to my cabin door. When he sets me down, he grabs my chin, his hand strong but careful. He turns my head this way and that, then pats down my arms. "Did he hurt you?" he asks when he seems to find nothing out of place.

That throws me. I had just been hanging out with Dylan at the helm, but Matthew is acting like I'd been under attack. "Of course not!" I take Matthews restless hands in mine. "Matthew, what's going on?" His eyes refuse to meet mine, so I pull him into my cabin. He swallows, and I make him sit on the bed before I close the door. When we're totally alone, I stride over to him and lift his chin so he's looking right at me. "Matthew, you have to tell me what's wrong."

He reaches out to me, hesitates for a moment, and then wraps his arms around my waist. He rests his head against my now bare belly, then sighs. I've never been this close to Matthew. Every one of our previous interactions had been careful, and he's never initiated any sort of intimate contact. I use this moment to slowly and carefully untie his hair, brushing through the tangled, salty strands and wrapping the band around my wrist. His hair is so unbelievably soft, despite the sea air. He groans when I use my nails to scratch his scalp as I continue to brush. Finally, he sighs and pulls away from me.

"Serenity, I need you to be careful around Dylan," he says. His dark eyes bore into mine, like this is the most important thing he's ever said.

"Why? What is so bad about Dylan?" I demand.

Matthew sucks in a deep breath, then pulls me to sit beside him. "Dylan is different than the rest of us," he starts. "You know by now that all dragons are born with some sort of special power. Mine is healing. Liam's is mind reading, but only for dragons. Adrian can read auras." I nod. Yes, I know all this already. "But we haven't told you Dylan's power."

He looks at me, waiting, but I don't say anything. It's almost like he's giving me the chance to change my mind, but I refuse to be afraid anymore. My fear of these dragons has almost ruined everything too many times to count, but, if I'm the lost princess they seem to think I am, then I will not hide. Not again.

"Dylan is human-born. Like Adrian. Like... me," he says. "And Liam."

Nobody told me all that. My mouth pops open in surprise. All of them had human parents? I wait for him to continue.

"He was found as a baby, but the team who found him had to be careful. When he was born, he killed his mother, and then his father. And the nurse in the hospital. After that, all the humans refused to touch him."

Wait, what? Dylan killed people? When he was a baby? That doesn't make any sense.

"Dylan's power is unique, but it's also dangerous. He sucks the life force out of those he touches."

I shake my head. "He's touched me, and I'm fine," I argue. Matthew must be making this up. There's no way Dylan could hurt someone like that.

"He can control it now, but when he was young, it happened to everyone he touched. He wasn't found by dragons until he was two, and he'd taken the life from a dozen people. Everyone knew not to touch him at that point, but mistakes happened." Matthew runs his hands through his hair like he's going to pull it back up, but he glances at me to find the ponytail holder still on my wrist.

"Poor Dylan," I breathe. "It must have been so lonely for him."

Matthew evaluates my face, confusion in his eyes. "Right. I guess it probably was." He turns to look out the window, but there's nothing to see but darkness. It will be hours before the sun comes up. I take his hand and twine our fingers together. "The queen—your mother—thought that he showed potential. She kept him in the palace and taught him to control his powers, but then, when he turned twelve, he was sent on missions."

"Twelve?" I ask. That's far too young for a boy to go on any sort of mission, and, from what the guys have told me, missions are dangerous.

Matthew nods. "He became an excellent killer. He would take out groups of hunters in a night, just from touching them. He was great at it, and he enjoyed it. At nineteen, he joined our group." Finally, Matthew's eyes meet mine again. They've gone from stoic to pleading. "He's dangerous, Serenity. I've never seen anyone so terrifying. The only reason we allow him to be around you is because Adrian keeps him on a tight leash. Unattended, though..." he trails off, and I squeeze his hand. "Serenity, just promise me you won't be alone with him."

I shake my head. "But you said he can control it. He isn't going to hurt me, Matthew." I refuse to believe that Dylan could do something so horrible, at least to me. He's *good*. I can feel it in my heart.

Matthew sighs with resignation. Is there somehow more to this gruesome story? "When he was twenty-two, Dylan was in love with a girl. A half-dragon girl named Siobhan." A painful lump forms in my throat, and I swallow. "He lost control, and she died."

I gasp, covering my mouth with my free hand. Tears spring to my eyes.

Matthew's voice becomes shaky. "Please, Serenity, stay away from Dylan."

He looks so sad and terrified that I nod, pulling him close to me. I have no intention of actually staying away from Dylan, but at this moment, I want nothing more than to make Matthew feel safe.

"We should get some sleep," I say. "It's the middle of the night."

He pulls me tighter, and I sigh against him.

"Can I sleep in here?" he mumbles.

I smile and tighten my arms around him. "I would like that."

CHAPTER FOURTEEN
SERENITY

When I awaken to a rattling sound and the sun streaming in directly above me. Matthew's arm is thrown across my chest, weighing me down. I tuck his disheveled hair out of his face, and he stirs, opening his eyes slowly.

"Morning, sleepyhead," I say. He groans and pulls me close to him, burying his face in my neck. His breath tickles, and I have to shove away from him while giggling. "I'm going to see what's going on."

He mumbles something indiscernible, and I pat him on his head before heading up into the sunlight. The first thing that I notice is land. A huge piece of land has carved itself out of the horizon, dozens or perhaps hundreds of boats moored through the harbor. Are we at Draecus Island already?

"Morning, Serenity," Dylan says with his usual cheerful grin, but there's a tightness to it. I stride over and fix his wind-blown hair. Despite what I told Matthew, I won't stay away from Dylan. I don't believe even a little bit that he would hurt me.

"Did you get any sleep at all?" I ask, and he looks away and shrugs.

"Serenity, can you help me with this?" Liam calls from the bow. I give Dylan an apologetic smile and journey across the boat. Liam is standing in an open storage hatch, and there are lines and boat parts and totes piled outside.

"Where are we?" I ask, taking the small plastic tote he hands me.

"Puerto Plata," he says, leaning down and rummaging for something else.

"The Dominican Republic?" I ask. This is where Jenna, my roommate, is from. Her parents immigrated to New York when she was just a baby. I look back toward the land, almost as if I could learn more about her just from being nearby.

"Yeah," Liam says, handing me a heavy rod of some sort. I set it to the side. "We're getting supplies for the last leg of the journey. Traveling through magical portals requires a lot of work and precision, so we're visiting some of the dragons who live here."

"Don't we need to check into the country or something?" I ask. I don't have a passport, something I should have considered before making this trip. Will I get arrested and sent back to New York?

He shakes his head. "Diplomatic Immunity. The Firefly is a royal vessel." He gestures at the mast, and I squint at the flags at the very top. I still have no idea what they look like, but Liam seems confident enough in their meaning.

"What are you doing now?" I ask, changing the subject.

He frowns, disappearing into the hole for a moment before popping back up. "Trying to find a spare part for the water maker. It's going out and I don't want to have to order in."

I nod, although I'm not really sure what a water maker is. I guess I haven't learned nearly enough about the boat considering I've been living on it for what feels like forever. In fact, when I think back to my life in New York, it feels like a million years ago rather than days.

"Ah-hah!" he says, holding up a plain hunk of metal that means nothing to me. I then proceed to pass back all the boxes, setting the part behind me.

"I want to go with," I say. "To meet these other dragons."

He pauses while setting down the final tote, then turns to look at me. "I don't know that that's a good idea," he says, heaving himself out of the hole. I move back so he has space, then he helps me to stand. A breeze blows my hair in my face, and he brushes it away before I have the chance.

"Why not?" I ask indignantly. It's hard to be too mad, though, when his hands are on me.

"It's not safe," he says. "There could be hunters, and we are trying to hide your existence from the rest of the world until we reach the palace." His lips swipe across my lips, and my breath stops. With the barest touch of his lips, I am completely immobilized. "Besides," he whispers against my skin, "I don't want to share you any more than I already have to." His hand moves from my hair and down, brushing over my throat and resting on my collarbone. He rubs with his thumb, and my eyes drift shut, the sun shining brightly through my eyelids.

I shake my head to get out of this stupor. "I'm not waiting here," I insist, scrunching his shirt in my fists.

He groans and looks away. "You're impossible, you know that?"

I nod. "I try my hardest."

Adrian pokes his head out of the galley door at that moment. "Ready to go, Liam?" he asks.

Liam looks at me, then takes my hand before nodding at Adrian. "Ready."

It feels a lot weirder than I expected to be back on land. My feet wobble, and my head swims like I'm still on the boat.

"You'll get used to it," Adrian says, holding me close. Liam doesn't seem pleased, but he allows it. Dylan and Matthew are still on the Firefly, preparing for the final leg of our journey. I'd asked both of them if they were going, but Adrian had shut down the hopeful look on Dylan's face immediately. I'll have to have a talk with Adrian about that at some point.

We rent a small car, and Liam follows the GPS through the city and up to a house with an iron fence around it. It's bigger than I expected, and my heart races. What will these dragons be like? If they're anything like mine, I have good reason to be nervous.

The earth-skinned middle-aged woman who opens the door is the last thing I expect. I just get a glimpse of her before Adrian moves in front of me on the narrow walkway from the driveway to the front door. She's tall for a woman, and despite her wild black hair, t-shirt, and swim shorts, there's something regal about her that makes me back against Liam for comfort.

"Mr. Byrne," the woman says with a Spanish accent, her strong voice surprised. "How nice to have you here. Come in, come in."

I follow Adrian in, and my eyes dart to meet the woman's as Liam keeps a steady hand on my upper arm.

"Ah," she says, her face breaking out into a knowing smile. "You've found another one!" She wraps me in a warm, motherly hug like nothing I've ever known. I sink into her arms and sigh. I don't know her from Eve, but the welcoming gesture is enough for me. Not even my own mother has ever been so affectionate with me. "Welcome home," she mumbles into my hair, and tears spring to my eyes.

"Thank you," I whisper back, trying to keep

the shake out of my voice.

After another moment, Adrian speaks, breaking us apart. "Serenity, meet Elena. She's part of the Basili Clan, and she and her husbands live here part of the year."

Elena nods, then looks me up and down. I'm still wearing a swimsuit, and I cross my arms over my bare stomach, suddenly self conscious. Should I be more dressed up for this meeting? "You seem hungry. Have these boys not been feeding you?"

At the same time that Liam scoffs, a laugh bursts out of me. "No, they have. I just didn't think about it this morning."

She shakes her head, and her eyes follow the way Liam's hand moves possessively to my waist. "Well, I'll let Oscar know to prepare another few plates. We were just getting ready to eat before our siesta."

I smile, about to take her up on her offer, when Adrian cuts in. "Actually, we have to be going. I just need those spells for our crossing."

Elena's easy going demeanor changes just slightly, her lips tightening into a line. "Fine. But I expect to hear that you've fed this girl after returning to the boat. If not, I will have a word with your mother."

Adrian laughs lightly, and the mood shifts from tension into an easy camaraderie. After that, the morning moves quickly. I'm introduced to Oscar and Johnny, a pair of men that seem to gravitate toward Elena. They seem to notice how the guys are always near me, a hand on my arm or my waist or my shoulder. I can't help but lean into their touches, and I should feel embarrassed—especially half-dressed as I am—but I just feel cared for.

We're at the house for less than half an hour by the time we're rushed out the door and heading back to the harbor.

The rest of the afternoon is spent preparing for the final crossing, although I notice Dylan seems to be avoiding me. Every time I enter a different part of the boat, he just happens to be leaving. It frustrates me, but it's not like I can talk to him if I can't get close to him. Maybe I'll follow Matthew's advice after all, if only because Dylan clearly doesn't want to be around me, either.

CHAPTER FIFTEEN
SERENITY

Matthew doesn't sleep in my room again to-night, and the sea tosses the boat around so much I can't fall back to sleep. I haven't gotten sick since day one, but now, my stomach churns. When I'd taken the boat ride in New York, the captain had told me to keep my eyes on the hori-zon, so I climb up out of my cabin, through the galley, and past the front doors to sit on one of the trampolines. I wrap a hand around the same cable as before, watching the boat slice through the choppy night water.

I don't even realize I've got company until a

familiar Irish voice says, "Serenity?"

I snap my head over to see Dylan lounging in one of the chairs that's bolted into the hull less than fifteen feet away from me. He's wearing a black jacket with a zip-up hoodie below it, the hood obscuring his features. For a moment, I think he might bolt, but instead, when he stands, he strides easily over to me. For Dylan, it's like we're not even on a moving vessel. I envy his grace.

"Hello," I say, leaning into him when he sits close enough to touch.

Instead of reciprocating, though, he flinches away. "Serenity, I can't. *We* can't."

I shake my head, a light laugh floating out of me and away with the wind. "Why, because Adrian says so?" I stare into his eyes, and he brushes his hand through his hair in frustration, his hood falling back.

"You don't understand," he replies. His voice is strained now, and his eyes dart back toward the galley. I know what he's really looking at, though. If Adrian knew Dylan and I were alone together, all hell would break loose. Mostly for Dylan, it seems.

I narrow my eyes at him. "I don't think you'd hurt me. I don't care what Matthew or Adrian or anyone else says."

He turns away from me at that moment, choosing to stare over the moon-lit water instead. We hit a particularly rough wave, and I hold even tighter to the cable, the only thing really keeping me from falling overboard. If I fell in, would I ever be found in the inky-black sea? The water sprays across my face in a gentle mist, and I shiver.

"Don't do this to yourself," Dylan says, still not looking at me. "You may be able to have anyone you want, but you shouldn't want me."

"Why not?" I say, my voice rising a good few levels. I don't even care if Adrian hears me. Hell, the whole boat could wake up for all I care. "Because you're dangerous? Or do you just not want me? If that's the case…" My words fade. I hadn't even considered that as a possibility until I said the words, and I choke, turning to the sea ahead instead of Dylan's face. It's selfish of me to want all of them. In my heart, I know that. But….

"God, Serenity," he says, his voice suddenly much closer. A gentle hand takes my face, turning me toward him. "Of course I want you." Then, much to my surprise, he presses his lips to mine. Unlike the desperate kisses with Adrian or the teasing kisses with Liam, this one is soft, careful. A question.

Is this okay?

Is it safe?

I lean into him, tangling my fingers in his silky-smooth hair. I can't help but press my body against his, and the blanket falls away. If I weren't sitting on it, it would fly off the boat in the wind. I shiver at the chilly night air that caresses my skin. I didn't change out of my bikini from this afternoon, and now, out in the cold, I regret that decision.

Dylan moves his hands down my arms, then to my waist. My breath catches in my throat when he traces tiny circles on the sensitive patch of skin right above my hip bone, the part right on the edge of my bikini.

Another shiver wracks my body and ruins the moment, though, and he pulls away. "We should get you inside," he mumbles, pulling the blanket up over my shoulders once again.

I shake my head, not in disagreement, but to clear the flood of thoughts and feelings that have invaded. "Are you gonna run away from me again?" I ask, tightening the blanket around myself like it can shield me from his response. He glances toward the helm again, and I reach up and caress his cheek.

He sighs and leans into my touch, pulling his

hand up to mine. "What if they know?" he asks.

I frown. "Then they can deal with me. If I have any say in the matter, then I want you." I pause. "No, I *need* you. All of you."

He sucks in a breath, and a shudder runs through his body. "I'm dangerous," he insists. His words are strained and feeble at this point, though.

"Not to me," I say, standing on wobbly feet and dragging him up with me. He doesn't resist, and he follows me through the doors. I catch Adrian's eye as he lounges on one of the benches at the helm, and he sits bolt upright when he notices Dylan with me. I give the smallest shake of my head, and his jaw sets. I'm sure there will be a discussion tomorrow, but right now, he doesn't fight me on my decision. Good.

When we make it downstairs to my cabin door, Dylan hesitates once again.

"Please," I say. "I can't be alone tonight."

He looks at the stairs like he's planning his escape, then back to me. He swallows, his Adam's Apple bobbing. How could someone so pretty and innocent looking be the ruthless killer everyone claims him to be? I lift a hand and brush the hair that's fallen over his eyes, but he still doesn't look at me.

"Dylan?" I ask, and his eyes finally meet mine, something inside them alight with fire.

He sighs and leans down swiftly, pressing his lips to mine, his need consuming me like he's drowning and I'm air. I groan into his kiss, and he presses me up against the cabin door. Trapped in his want, I can't fathom the momentary idea I had that he didn't want me. I fumble behind me for the door, sliding it open so we can stumble back to my bed. He doesn't hesitate this time, following me desperately inside. He doesn't even take the time to close the door again before stumbling after me into the bed.

"Why can't I resist you?" he asks, kissing messily down my neck, my blonde hair spread behind me like a halo on the bed.

I don't answer, just tangle my fingers through his hair, breathing in everything that is Dylan.

Just before I can beg him for more, for all of him, a shot of electricity bursts through me, light dancing behind my eyes. I cry out, and my hands catch fire like never before.

Dylan sits up, and his eyes turn from lustful to concerned. When he sees the fire on my hands, he picks me up before I can put my arms down and set any of the covers on fire.

"I'm sorry," I gasp, clenching my fists desperately to try to fix the situation. My face heats, not from the fire of my hands, but shame and embarrassment. I've never lost control like this around someone outside my family, and, in the back of my mind, there's still that bit of fear that my mother drilled into me. Nobody will love me like this. *Worthless. Monster.*

With no regard for the flames, Dylan takes my hands in his. "Serenity, breathe."

I shake my head, a gasp coming out as I try to tell the fire to just go away, but it doesn't listen to me. The sleeves of Dylan's sweatshirt catch fire, but only up to his wrists that are outside the circle of flame. "I can't. I can't stop it," I sob, and the flames grow brighter.

"Serenity," Dylan says, his voice going from gentle too stern. "You can. You know you can. I just need you to breathe. You're okay."

I suck in a breath, my whole body shaking as I try to control the flames.

"Good," he says. "Again. Breathe. Focus on your breath and my voice."

Tears fall from my eyes, evaporating the moment they get too close to the flames in front of me. I breathe in again, letting Dylan's words wrap around me. "Can you say my name again?" I ask.

"Serenity," he says. The way my name twists

over his Irish tongue is irresistible, and I breathe out slowly. "Serenity," he whispers, leaning in closer to me. I look into his eyes, and he breathes slowly with me. "Serenity," he breathes, and the flames finally go out.

He smiles, his eyes sad. So sad. I understand the look on his face now, the one I've been trying so hard to puzzle out. The shame, the worthlessness that I've felt my entire life because of my powers. It's the exact same way he's always felt. I lean forward, pressing my forehead to his. "Dylan, I'm so sorry."

He lets out a breathless, humorless laugh. "For what? You did nothing wrong."

I carefully lift his chin so that he's looking me in the eyes, though I'm still half afraid that I'll set him on fire. "I'm sorry you've been treated like a monster."

With that, his face crumples, and he puts his head on my shoulder.

"I'm sorry," I say. "I never want you to feel that way again."

I tell him how sorry I am over and over and over, stroking his hair while his tears soak my shoulder. Has he ever been held like this? With true, fearless affection? From the moment he was born, he was treated like a monster.

Like me.

I vow, right then and there, that I will keep him safe. Eventually, after breaking through his walls, he will know to never doubt my feelings for him. I will not fear him, and those who do will not hurt him.

CHAPTER SIXTEEN
ADRIAN

I stay at the helm the rest of the night. If I were released from this self-imposed prison, I would break down Serenity's door to make sure that Dylan could not harm her. I've seen far too much of what he can do, and he will not harm a hair on her head. Still, the look she'd given me had frozen me to my seat. I could do nothing but obey, and now I'm torturing myself with wonder at what could be going on down there.

If Dylan were to lose control, Serenity could be gone in less time than it takes me to get to her cabin.

"Chilly out," Matthew says, appearing like a spirit from the shadows. I nod, my jaw ticking. He tosses a blanket at me, which I catch with one hand. Serenity's aura is still stable, but that could change at a moment's notice. Matthew sighs loudly and collapses on the bench beside me, stretching his arms over his head with an obnoxiously loud groan.

"How can I be calm when Serenity is willingly putting herself in danger?" I demand, my hands heating with tension and fury. I would do anything to keep Serenity safe, and it's almost like she's throwing it in my face. Still, I can't say no to my Princess. She is my everything, and I am at her total mercy.

Matthew shakes his head, his hair falling across his unreadable features. His aura shows that of turmoil, though. He's just as nervous as I. "You need to trust her a bit," he says. This surprises me, because Matthew has shown no real signs of believing in Serenity. He has been spending a lot of time with her since we left Miami, though. Does he feel the same bond that Liam seems to feel? That I feel?

Instead of asking, I lean back on the seat. The wheel of the catamaran turns and twitches as the computer tells it what to do to stay on course, and the sails bulge with the gentle breeze moving us along.

"I think," Matthew says slowly, "that you may not be the only one."

I make a noncommittal noise. Is he still talking about Serenity involving herself with Dylan?

"I was in the palace, too," Matthew continues. When I glance over at him, he's leaning forward, elbows on his knees and chin resting on his folded hands. I wait for him to finish his thought, although I know exactly where it's headed. "When the queen bound you together. We all were. What if…"

He stops then, moving his focus out to sea as the words catch in his throat. His aura changes from tense to just plain anxious, but I don't speak up. I already know he's right. Of course he is. We've all felt it, this inexplicable connection to the woman I found in the snowy streets of New York not long ago. She is bound to us. All of us.

"What if the queen bound us all together on purpose?" he finally asks.

And there it is. The question we've all been wondering, the question that answers so much. Why I was able to find her in New York, why Liam found her in the forest, why Matthew was drawn to heal her, why she has no fear of Dylan despite his sordid past.

I sigh, closing my eyes under the weight of the night. This mission was supposed to be simple. It was supposed to just be the possibility of finding a random dragon shifter. It wasn't supposed to turn into all this.

My heart aches as I lie there silently, unable to voice the turbulence making its way through my mind.

"So you feel it, too," Matthew says, my silence apparently enough of a response for him. He sighs with frustration. "Why is nothing ever as easy as it's supposed to be? I didn't ask to be bound to a mate. I was a child, for fuck's sake!" He begins to pace, his footsteps reverberating into my seat. At the rate that he's moving, he's going to wake up the whole yacht.

"We all were," Liam says, his voice quiet and calm as ever as he appears in the doorway. He's always the reasonable one, the stable one. Matthew and I may be closer, but Liam is the one who can always calm him down with reason. "I understand the frustration, but we have a duty. We have to keep her safe, to ensure she ascends the throne in her mother's place." He shrugs. "It's not like binding mates is uncommon. It protects the species, after all."

He has a point. There are so few dragons as it is. If male dragons were constantly fighting each other for a mate, there would be a total blood-bath. It's easier to just bind us when we're young so that it doesn't come to that.

"Why four human-borns, though?" Matthew asks, his frustration still evident even without his aura seeping into me. "Wouldn't the queen want her daughter to mate with purebloods or something?"

I frown. Matthew's adopted father is a pure-blood who didn't know of Matthew's lineage before adopting him. "Careful," I say with a growl in my throat. I have been trying to get rid of Matthew's inherited prejudice against humans for years, but his father beat it into him. Those scars are difficult to heal.

He glares at me, then looks to Liam, who shakes his head marginally. Liam is still in his pajamas, a pair of flannel pants and a ripped gray t-shirt. In the moonlight, his freckles stand out like blood spatter against his deathly pale skin. Liam may be quiet, but he is truly the most dangerous of any of us. Dylan can kill with a single touch, but Liam can destroy you from the inside out. Matthew knows this, and it's why he listens to him.

"Whatever," Matthew says, then storms over

the edge, transforming and shredding his clothes. He soars up like he's trying to reach the moon, and I'm sure he'll fly over the boat for a while until he cools down. His dark form would be indiscernible if he weren't blocking out the stars that are brighter in the middle of the ocean than anywhere else in the world.

I sigh and shake the sparks out of my hands, and they fall harmlessly, disappearing before they can even touch anything.

"You should get some sleep," Liam says, watching the sky pale marginally at the edges of the eternal sea. His voice is light as the wind, but as serious as always.

I shake my head. "I'm fine." Even if she and Dylan are bound together, I won't be able to sleep until I see her again.

One of Liam's eyebrows prick up. "You know, she doesn't have to be alone with him."

I bite my bottom lip. It's true that many dragon women share a bed with all their mates, but Serenity wasn't raised as a dragon. She was raised in the human world where things like this are still considered taboo.

"Go to her," Liam insists, sitting at the captain's chair and pulling out his earbuds. "She's been gone our whole lives. There's no time to waste with her."

I sigh. He's right. I've been waiting my whole life to reunite with Serenity. Many dragons grow up with their mates, but because of the war, we've been separated far longer than is normal. I feel like I've been missing a part of my soul, and Serenity fills that gap. If she and Dylan are bound as well, then I must trust him to keep her safe. And I can't let my reservations get in the way of our happiness.

"Fine," I say, abandoning him at the helm. I pad through the ship, perfectly aware of everyone on board as well as Matthew flying through the air. I go until I reach the hall where Serenity and my cabins are. Instead of going to my own room, I knock gently on her door. When Dylan answers it, his face and aura both darken, not with anger, but with fear and sadness. Serenity is lying on the bed, her eyes fluttering open, but she doesn't sit up. She must be exhausted, and I've woken her. "May I join you both?" I ask as casually as possible.

Dylan relaxes significantly, and Serenity's face forms a placid smile. She opens her arms, and I join her on the bed, climbing over top of her to be on her other side. Dylan only hesitates for a moment, but he lies down as well. Serenity's aura flows through me, peaceful and content. I trace my fingers through her silky blonde hair until we all fall asleep.

CHAPTER SEVENTEEN
SERENITY

When I wake up, the first thing I notice in the blue light of early morning is the smothering heat. I open my eyes to find myself sandwiched between Adrian and Dylan, and my body is slick with sweat despite the lack of a blanket and proper clothing. I clamber over Dylan to get out of bed, and he barely even reacts, still far too tired to get up. He must have been holding so much tension inside him, and now he seems finally able to truly relax.

I dig through a drawer in the closet, picking an oversized t-shirt and shorts to wear over a string bikini. I exit the room as quietly as possible.

Changing in the head is a test of my acrobatics, and the tossing of the boat in the rough water certainly doesn't help. I stumble a few times, even managing to fall on my ass in the shower. I suck in a sharp breath as pain radiates through my body. Yup, definitely bruised my tailbone doing that trick.

Finally, though, I make it out alive. I'm pretty sore, so I'm glad when I see that Matthew is at the helm.

"Morning," I say with a yawn. He frowns. Great. Not this again. "You seem grumpy. Been up all night?"

He huffs. "Something like that." He's leaning back in the captain's chair, so I walk behind him and carefully untie his hair. He may be pissy this morning, but he doesn't fight me as I brush my fingers through, methodically working out the knots that have wormed their way in. "You should probably deep condition as long as we're at sea," I say. The conditioner that their mysterious assistant bought me has worked wonders, and my hair has a glow to it that I've never seen before.

"Why are you up so early?" Matthew asks, his voice distant. He groans as I scratch his scalp, leaning his head back so his brown, wavy hair cascades over the back of the chair.

I shrug even though he isn't looking at me. "It got a bit hot in my room. I feel good, though."

He doesn't reply to that, and I continue on with my mission of detangling his hair. When it's as smooth as I can get it without some serious product, I begin to braid the sides.

"What are you doing?" he asks. It's clear that he's exhausted, and my fingers moving through his hair seem to be lulling him into sleep.

"Giving you viking braids," I say matter-of-factly. "I think they'd look good on you."

He sighs but doesn't say anything more. The sky goes from gray-blue to purple to pink, and Liam takes his place in the galley. He waves at me with a spatula before cracking some eggs, and I wave back.

As the sun turns the sea and clouds golden, I catch strands of golden-blonde in Matthew's hair, and the sight makes me smile.

"I have a good reason to dislike humans, you know," Matthew admits. His voice startles me—I thought he'd fallen asleep.

"You do?" I ask. I don't totally believe him, but I'm trying to get him to open up to me.

He shrugs half-heartedly but doesn't open his

eyes. "It's just hard for me to trust them. When I was a baby, my parents saw me transform. So they abandoned me."

I nod, then realize that he can't actually see me. "I'm sorry," I say.

He shakes his head and sits up just as I tie off the last braid. Now, instead of his hair falling all over, each side has two braids, one large and one small. The top center is in a huge loose braid that I learned to do on a YouTube video dive, and it stays in place without hairspray because of the salt in the air. I only wish I had beads and such to tie into his braids to finish the look.

"They left me in the garbage," he says, his words coming out strained as he stands and turns to me, placing his hands on my upper arms. I gasp and cover my mouth with my hands.

"Oh, god. Matthew I..." There's nothing I can say, though. Nothing to fix how he feels. How he must have felt knowing how terrified I was when he transformed. Not only did other humans hurt him in the past, but I myself proved that humans would be terrified of dragons. I may have magic powers, but seeing that had freaked me out beyond belief.

I walk around the seat that separates us and fold myself in his arms. His hands are outstretched for a moment, and his heart thumps wildly in my ear. After what feels like an eternity, though, he wraps his arms around me, resting his chin on top of my head. After a moment, the sliding glass door opens, and Liam's warm presence arrives.

"Breakfast," he says gently, and I turn my head to watch him place bowls on the outside table. Before he goes inside to do more preparation, he leans forward and kisses me on the cheek. I flush and pull away from Matthew, who sighs and goes to the table. When I take my seat on one of the benches, he sits on the other. I frown, but Liam is back outside with more food before I can comment.

"Good morning, Serenity," he says. The delicate way he says my name makes me tingle, and I have to take a bite of food as an excuse to not reply. I know if I were to say anything, it wouldn't come out half as eloquent. He joins me on my bench, kissing me on the side of the head before working on his own breakfast. "I hope you slept well."

I stammer out a "yes," then continue to eat the breakfast rice bowl he'd made for me. His left hand rests on my knee, and my stomach ties itself in knots. I do my best to think about the food in front of me, the beauty of the sunrise over the waves, anything other than the way Liam's simple touch peels away my layers of self control.

He muffles a laugh, which is when I realize that he's tormenting me on purpose. He either knows every impure thought of mine, or I'm just shouting in his brain about food and the ocean. His laugh turns into a cough, and Matthew glances up, pricking an eyebrow.

"You dying, Liam?" he asks, his eyes darting to me.

Liam waves him off with a smile, and I feel myself growing hot.

"I think I'm gonna eat upstairs," I announce. To escape the table, I have to climb over Liam, and he squeezes my thigh much higher than I'm used to as I make my way over him. I suck in a breath. "Liam," I hiss, lightly smacking his arm with the back of my hand when I'm finally past him.

Matthew rolls his eyes. "I'll join you. Liam, man the helm."

Liam's humor turns into a pout, and I laugh at him. Still, I give him a light kiss on the forehead before following Matthew to the upper deck.

The sails are full and the horizon is clear up here, and I take in a deep breath of the salt air. I desperately need to calm myself. Matthew takes my bowl and sets it on the table, and before I can go to sit beside him, he pulls me into his lap, my legs straddling either side of his muscled thighs.

"Matthew, what are you—"

My words are cut off when he tangles a hand in my hair, his lips crashing into mine. I let out a surprised moan, then rest my hands on his chest as I let myself sink into his embrace.

"God, Serenity," he groans, pulling my hair to tilt my head back. He trails kisses down my neck, and I let out a gasp when he nips at my sensitive skin. "You have no idea what you do to me."

The hardness pressing into me gives me an idea, and I gasp again when he grinds up against me. It's been far too long since I've gotten laid, and I'm not sure how much longer I can last. My biggest issue with keeping a boyfriend back home was that I had a much larger libido than the men I'd date, so I got bored easily. Not to mention trying to hide my magical powers. Now, with Matthew here and clearly ready, my self control crumbles.

"Please," I beg, my voice hardly more than a breath in the wind. He tightens his arms around me, pressing his face into my neck and inhaling. Clearly I'm not the only one having issues controlling myself. I trail my hands down his chest, then tuck my fingers into the waistband of his swim trunks.

Instantly, his hand in my hair releases so that he can move it around, lifting my shirt over my chest to reveal the skimpy black bikini I'm wearing in lieu of underwear. Without preamble, he shoves the stretchy fabric out of the way and takes my nipple into his mouth.

"Fuck," I gasp, my hands bunching into fists as I ride him, matching his body's rhythm as well as I can. Just as I'm about to reach the edge, though, he pushes me away, pulling his lips from my body. I tremble as I stand in front of him. "Matthew," I breathe, but before I can say anything more, he pulls my shirt over my head, his eyes burning every piece of my body that they touch. I fumble to help him remove his shirt, and his toned body is in front of me. I'm almost scared to touch him, like he might run away or decide this is wrong.

He keeps his eyes on mine as he reaches for my waist, slowly unbuttoning my shorts before shimmying them down my hips. I'm still wearing my disheveled bikini, but I feel more naked than I've ever felt in front of a man.

"Is this okay?" he asks, running his fingers gently over my ribs and waist, my skin turning electric with his touch. I swallow and nod. Unlike last night with Dylan, I focus on my fire to ensure I don't light up this time.

He smiles, continuing down until his fingers are tucked into the strings that tie both sides of my bikini bottoms together. With one quick movement, they're untied. A shiver runs through me, although I couldn't possibly be cold right now. He puts his steady hands on my hips, standing to tower over me and kiss me once again. I take this opportunity to pull his swim trunks down past his hips, taking his manhood in one hand. Fuck, he's big. Bigger than any of the men I've slept with recently, at least. Possibly the biggest I've had. He groans, rolling his hips once again.

"Sit back down," I say, finally finding my voice. He does as I say, pulling me along with him. I stroke his cock steadily, watching his face fall into deep elation. His hands become clumsy, and he reaches to rub his palm against my slit. His hands are so hot that it feels like his skin is on fire, and I rub myself on his hand. When I whimper with need, he parts me and puts two fingers inside me. "Matthew," I moan, tossing my head back. The wind whips my hair around me, and it's almost like flying.

"You're fucking soaked, Serenity," he mumbles, his movements becoming more deliberate.

The heel of his hand rubs just over my clit, and I tangle the hand not on his cock through his hair just to keep my balance. If it weren't for him holding me up, I may honestly collapse with the waves of pleasure rolling through me. It builds and builds, but he removes his fingers just as I'm approaching orgasm.

"God damn it, Matthew," I cry. Why is he doing this to me? Before I can do much more, though, he guides me onto his cock, and I lower myself down. Another cry rips out of me. By now everyone on the boat must know what we're doing, but I can't control my volume with him. I have to adjust to the size of him filling me, but he doesn't give me long before grabbing my hips and moving me over him to the rhythm of the boat rolling over the ocean.

I should be worried about someone walking in on us, about being exposed, but my mind and body are alight with Matthew. I tangle my fingers through the parts of his hair that remain unbraided, then kiss him like I'm drowning and he's oxygen.

The feeling of release builds inside me once again, and I clench my thighs around Matthew. This time, he finally allows the orgasm to wash over me. I have to pull away from the kiss to cry out a final time, and Matthew rakes his nails down my back.

When I'm finally finished, my body is left trembling and exhausted, and I slump to rest my forehead on his shoulder.

"You are stunning, Princess," he mumbles into my hair, tracing gentle patterns over my spine. A shiver runs over my bare body, and he wraps me into a warming hug. "We should probably get you inside."

My heart trips over itself as I realize that everyone must have heard what we were doing up here. I didn't care in the moment, but my face heats at the idea of facing the rest of the guys now.

Matthew runs a hand through my hair. "It's alright," he promises. He can't read minds or auras, but with his healing powers, he must be able to feel my body's reaction to the idea of interacting with everyone else moments after the greatest orgasm of my life. I groan when I pull myself off of him, then scramble to get dressed as well as I can in my state. When I turn back to him, Matthew is fully dressed once again.

He reaches his hand to me, but before I can take it, a deafening crack sounds, like lightning striking the boat.

I gasp as the electric feeling rolls through me,

my hands bursting into flame for just an instant before going out.

"Serenity?" Matthew asks, but I can't respond. My jaw is locked shot as pain reverberates through my body, my bones cracking and shifting.

I look at him, and he gasps.

I want to ask him what's happening, but before I can, my body shifts.

CHAPTER EIGHTEEN
ADRIAN

None of us had considered the effect that entering Draecus territory would have on Serenity. She hasn't been here since she was a baby, and there's every chance she's never transformed in her life. I rush to the upper deck just in time to see a panicked dragon tangling herself in the mainsail, a roar shaking the sky.

"Serenity, I need you to calm down," Matthew shouts, but his eyes are wild with panic. Her glistening rose gold scales ripple as a shiver wracks her body. Her tail whips around as she continues to struggle, getting even more tangled in the sail.

"Fuck," I mutter. At that moment, another dragon launches into the air behind us. From the pale stripes on his bronze body, I recognize it as Liam. Now that she's in her dragon form, he can project his thoughts into her mind. When she sees his form, though, she recoils. Does she not realize that she looks similar to him?

Her head rears back, and her spiral horns pierce the sail. When she tries pulling back, her head is stuck. This releases a fresh wave of terror in her, and she yanks harder. The mast cracks at the force, and I have to dive out of the way to avoid getting knocked out by the boom.

God damn it.

I remove my clothes and transform as quickly as I can. If we can't calm her enough that she shifts back, we might as well find a way to restrain her.

Serenity, I project. *We need you to stop. Breathe. You're going to sink the boat.*

Her response is an incoherent mess of fear and confusion, so I launch into the air to get an idea of how bad the situation is from up high. Liam is still in front of her, but he doesn't seem to be having any luck. Dylan is the next to transform, rushing out just as the top deck snaps from the pressure, crashing down to destroy the main deck. Matthew is barely holding on, but he still doesn't transform.

I let out a scream that would shake the earth if we were close enough, and it should be enough to let the island know that there is a problem.

Matthew, tiny from this angle, stumbles over the broken deck, dodging debris and Serenity. He makes his way to her face, then places a hand on her.

Of course. In his dragon form, Matthew wouldn't be able to ground himself without sinking the entire boat. In his human form, though, he can force her to shift back using his powers.

Relax, Princess, I tell her as calmly as I'm able. Her body shakes and her wings writhe, but she doesn't toss her head or her claws.

Slowly, her body starts to change back, her wings retracting into her shoulder blades and bones shifting back into a human form. When done purposefully, the process is quick and painless. This transformation, though, must be horribly painful. I float down and transform back into my human form just before reaching the destroyed deck.

Serenity's naked body trembles as she clings to Matthew, sobs bursting out of her. My heart shatters in my chest as I absorb every emotion she's feeling right now. The other two land short-ly after me, although Dylan tosses the destroyed mast and boom into the sea before turning hu-man again.

I tug on the swim trunks I'd been wearing be-fore the incident, although I have to shake some wood shards from the deck off them. Then, I shake off the t-shirt and help Serenity into it. Her sobbing has stopped, but her body is still shak-ing, and tears run down her face. She lets me put the shirt over her, then collapses into my arms.

I sigh and hold her close, tears welling up in my eyes as her emotions overwhelm me.

Now that the mast is gone, there's nothing on the boat to counterbalance the weight of the keels. As the waves move in, the boat thrashes about violently, but there's nothing we can do but wait. We could fly Serenity to the island, but her terror at seeing Liam transform had been enough to convince me that she's not in the emotional state for such a maneuver. So I hold her, and, as the sun begins to rise to the center of the sky for noon, a boat engine turns my head.

Throughout the day, I've spotted dragons ca-reening through the sky, but it seems that they've held off from landing near the boat, thank good-ness. We don't need more dragons to make the situation more terrifying for Serenity.

The boat approaching us is a small yacht, although I can't figure out from the distance who the driver is. It approaches carefully, circling a few times while Dylan and Liam shout instructions to keep the yacht from getting damaged by our unsalvageable catamaran. Serenity nestles even closer, which doesn't seem possible until she does it. Matthew is sitting nearby, his aura dim as exhaustion from the morning's task overtakes him. I know it requires a lot of energy for him to heal, but I didn't realize how much it would take out of him to force Serenity to shift back.

Finally, the boats are tethered together with several rubber bumpers between them. Liam and Dylan elect to stay on the Firefly, and Matthew and I make our way over to the other yacht. After he climbs over, I pass Serenity to him, and she nestles into him as easily as she had done for me. It makes sense, of course, based on what they'd been doing before Serenity transformed. The only thing that confuses me is how adamant Matthew had been that he didn't want her despite their bond.

The tender way he looks at her, though, keeps my mouth shut. He clearly cares deeply for her despite his words.

The driver of the yacht finally reveals himself, a shorter man with skin the color of ochre and tight gray and black dreads that fall down his back elegantly. A smile spreads across my face. "Henri," I call. I've known the queen's consort since I was a child. I climb over into the smaller yacht, wrapping an arm around him.

"And who do we have today?" Henri asks, watching Matthew carry her into the interior of the yacht.

My heart speeds up. We kept Serenity's presence a secret from Draecus on purpose. If a message had been intercepted, hunters or even rebels might have come after us. I didn't want to risk harm to her. "That's Serenity." I swallow the nerves building inside. "Princess Sérénité Amalia Claudette."

Her full name, which I haven't spoken aloud until now, leaves Henri speechless, and he looks at the doors where she just disappeared.

"Are you certain?" he asks, his voice dry. I nod. He shakes his head as if to clear his thoughts. "Well. I will alert the queen." He reaches for the CB radio at the helm, and I cover his hand with mine.

"I don't think it's wise," I say. "I fear she may still be in danger. If I hadn't found her the moment I did, she would not be alive. Messages are too easy to intercept."

Henri's eyes widen, and he hangs the hand-held radio back in place. "As you wish," he says. He starts the motor back up, and we make our way slowly toward the island. I have to adjust the bumpers and call instructions over to Dylan and Liam, but it goes fairly smoothly.

The island appears as we pass the second barrier, but, thankfully, this one has no effect on our powers. It's like driving through a fog, except the horizon goes from empty ocean to a huge island in the blink of an eye. The harbor has several boats, varying from small vintage sailboats to giant powered yachts. We'd left for our mission during the New Year, and plenty of dragons visit by sea rather than trying to fly in. Draecus Island is said to be the birthplace of all dragons, and many travel home for the holiday. Just a couple weeks ago, the harbor had been packed, boats moored and anchored so tight that only small dinghies could navigate between them.

Now, the boats left are spaced out well enough that we can limp the Firefly into the bay. As soon as we arrive, Dylan and Liam have to help with a haul out. If anyone can save any part of this wreckage, it's the marine mechanics of Draecus Island. With the amount of damage Serenity caused, though, I won't hold my breath.

The whole process is fairly quick, and before long, the yacht Henri brought is in the dock reserved for royal vessels—the one where we would have parked the Firefly had it not been destroyed. Liam and Dylan will meet us at the palace, as I watched them being taken from the shipyard into a black car.

I go into the galley of the yacht, then down to the master bedroom, knocking gently. Matthew opens the door, and I look past him to see Serenity asleep on the bed. Her cheeks are flushed, and her eyes are swollen from tears. My heart shatters all over again.

"I thought it was best to make her sleep," Matthew says, following my gaze. "Today has been a lot." I nod. That's a fair assessment.

I carry her up to the deck, and a royal guard has laid out the boarding ramp, so I'm able to carry her across without passing her to Matthew. She curls into my chest, her eyebrows scrunching together in confusion. Before I can ask him to, Matthew runs his fingers through her hair, and her sleep deepens once again.

"The queen is in council chambers all day," Henri says, leading us up the dock to the waiting car, a pearl white stretch SUV with the nation's flag, a violet piece of fabric with a dragon circling the royal crest. Matthew opens the door, and I buckle Serenity in, holding her so her head rests peacefully on my shoulder.

We pass through the winding streets of the morning city, the tinted windows protecting our identities from potential onlookers. The city is just starting to awaken, shops opening and parents taking their children for walks. We pass the sea turtle rescue just as they're unlocking their doors, and a woman and three men walk in, their two children sprinting excitedly past them. The sight sends a pang through my heart, and I can't help but wonder if that will be us someday as Serenity rests on my shoulder.

The drive to the castle is short, and the driver takes us directly to the rear entrance so we aren't visible from the street. I follow Henri into the castle, and Tomas, another of the queen's mates, meets us there. Last I heard, Phillip was off-island. I wonder if we'll see him soon now that the princess has returned?

"Another one?" he asks, watching Serenity's sleeping form. I realize with a start that she has the same elegant nose as Tomas, something I hadn't noticed until now.

Henri nods and puts a hand on Tomas's shoulder. "She's the princess," he says, and Tomas's jaw drops. He reaches out as if to touch her, then stops.

"It can't be..." he whispers, his eyes tracing her face. He must see himself in her features, though, something that should have been so obvious to me when I met her, because he nods.

"I think we should get her to bed," Matthew says slowly. Tomas is about to argue, but Henri's hand stops him. "She has had a shocking day, and waking around strangers would not help the situation."

Tomas nods. "I will notify the queen."

"I think that would be smart," I reply, shifting my weight. "I will take her to my quarters for now."

With that, the two men depart, and Matthew and I climb several sets of stairs and take one elevator to get to my room, a small suite in a distant nook of the castle. Out of all of us, I'm the only one who grew up on the palace grounds, although Matthew was here throughout our childhoods, as his adopted father is a general who spends a lot of time in the palace. I was brought to the palace with my parents when I was very young, although they have long since moved back to the human world. They never fit into dragon society, but they did what they thought was best for me to keep me safe. When the queen offered to bond me to her daughter, they'd enthusiastically agreed.

I set Serenity in the oversized bed, brushing her hair back with my fingers. "Alright," I say, "you can wake her."

Matthew is absolutely drained from the constant use of his powers, but he complies, taking one of her hands in his own. As Serenity's eyes flutter open, his close, and he collapses into the bed beside her.

"Adrian?" Serenity croaks, lifting a shaking hand to my face. I rest my cheek in her palm, her warmth reassuring in ways I cannot explain.

"You're safe," I say, covering her hand with my own. "You're in the palace."

She sucks in a breath and jolts up, jerking her hand away from me. The loss of her touch is worse than a slap, but I don't tell her that.

"Adrian," she breathes, "did I turn into a fucking dragon?"

CHAPTER NINETEEN
SERENITY

It can't be true.

I mean, it obviously is. I'd felt it. I'd transformed, my bones cracking and shifting until I was a fire-breathing monster. It hadn't seemed real, and I can hardly remember it all. The main thing I remember is the pain. My muscles are sore just thinking about it, and I keep my eyes on Matthew. Adrian reassured me that he'd be fine, that he just needs to sleep, but I'm worried about him.

"Serenity, will you say something?" Adrian pleads. I stop my restless pacing, glancing at him as he sits on the edge of the bed, concern etched across his features. I want to rub the crinkle in his forehead away, but I'm too anxious to stop moving. Every time I remember the feeling of shifting, my stomach drops, and my heart flutters like it's trying to fly out of my chest.

I shake my head, and, embarrassingly, hot tears sting at the corner of my eyes. I'd cried all morning after transforming, but that had been from the utter shock and pain of it all. I have no real reason to cry now, but I have to hold back the waves of emotion crashing at the gates of my self-control.

Adrian stands and strides purposefully to me, then places his hands on my shoulders, forcing me to stand in place. I look away, keeping my eyes on a vintage desk that's covered with paperwork.

"Serenity," he says. I bite my lip, so he puts a finger under my chin and turns my face to him. God, those brown eyes. I could get lost in them every day for the rest of my life. "I need you to breathe."

I suck in a breath but don't release it.

When someone knocks and opens the door, I jump half out of my skin, but it's just Liam and Dylan. Where have they been all morning?

"Serenity," Liam breathes, and I release the

breath just as my lungs begin to burn in protest. Although Adrian still has me, Liam comes up behind me and wraps his arms around my waist, burying his face in my neck. "I'm glad you're awake."

I relax into his hold, and Adrian sighs, releasing me. "Dylan," he says, "I need you to go find Serenity something to wear."

I'm still in Adrian's t-shirt, which fits me like a potato sack. It goes just past my butt, and if I were to raise my arms, everyone would get a highly inappropriate view.

"Yeah," Dylan says, although he looks more like he wants to reach out and touch me. If it weren't for Liam's iron grip around me, I'd go to him. He exits the room after a longing stare, and I take in another sharp breath.

"Breathe properly," Liam whispers, his lips tickling my throat in a way that makes me wonder how quickly he could go from a simple hug to running his fingers down my body, under the shirt, and then—

I clamp down on my thoughts, and he chuckles. I pull away. I can't focus while standing in his arms, so I go over to the bed and sit, covering my lap with the heavy comforter. "Whose room is this?" I ask. When we first came in, I had considered that it might be some sort of guest quarters, but it looks lived in.

Adrian frowns. "Stop changing the subject." *Ah. So it's his.*

"I like it," I say, ignoring his feeble order. Every time my thoughts go back to this morning's incident, I feel like I did that first day on the boat. Nauseated as hell. He seems to sense my discomfort, because he doesn't push the issue. Instead, he sits beside me, offering his arms as a peace offering. I nestle into them, and Liam collapses across the foot of the bed, head resting over Matthew's legs that hang off the end.

That's how we're positioned when Dylan returns, and Adrian shows me to the bathroom so I can change into the clothing he procured.

The clothes appear fairly basic—a knee-length white skirt with a gold and pink flower pattern, and a white lace top with a Peter Pan neckline. The underwear is plain and nude, which makes sense considering the pale color scheme. Still, when I put it on, the fabric is soft and luxurious, much like the clothes Mom had always refused to buy me from Bloomingdales. A price tag itches against my leg, and I tug it out and nearly choke at the four-figure price tag on the skirt. Is the gold pattern actual freaking gold or something? I leave the tag on just in case there's been a mistake and someone plans on returning the outfit, which is the only thing that makes sense.

"Adrian?" I call, opening the door a centimeter. His face appears, concern etched on his eyebrows.

"Yes, Princess?" The pet name still makes me blush, and I have to swallow the feelings welling up inside me right now.

"Can you button me up?" The back of the shirt has about a million little gold buttons, probably because of the unforgiving fabric.

He smiles. "Of course."

I hide behind the door as he comes in, although all the guys have seen me in far less on the boat. I can't help but glance at Matthew asleep on the bed when that thought crosses my mind. Yeah, a lot less than a skirt and long-sleeved shirt. I close the door to hide the lobster shade my face must have taken on by now.

"How are you feeling?" Adrian asks while he buttons me up, his fingertips brushing over the skin of my back and sending a shiver down my spine. I hold my hair up for him so it doesn't tangle or block him.

I swallow. "Fine."

"Nervous about meeting your mother?" he

asks.

Honestly, I've been in total denial about the whole situation. I've grown up with a distant, uncaring family. How will this woman be any different? She doesn't know me, and even the people who do know me don't seem to care about me at all.

Adrian cares, my brain supplies. *And Matthew. And Liam. And Dylan.*

"Definitely," I say just to shut the little voices up.

His body shifts, and he's suddenly pressed against my back. I try to step forward in shock, but the sink is keeping me in place. His lips brush the sensitive skin of my neck, and I gasp.

"You have nothing to worry about," he whispers. Then, he nips me right where my neck and shoulder meet, pulling a little moan out of me.

"Not right now," I force myself to say. "I don't want to ruin this outfit."

A deep laugh comes out of him, and he wraps an arm around my waist. His hips rub against my ass, the hardness in his pants so goddamn tempting that I clench my teeth to keep from crying out with need.

"Alright, Princess," he says, pulling away and leaving me to stand alone, the space between my thighs hot and sore and my mind a jumble.

God, damn it. How am I supposed to go on with everyone doing this to me? It has been mere hours since the incident on the boat, yet I'm hot and bothered just from the barest of touches from Adrian. And now I'm expected to meet with the queen.

My mother.

A shiver runs down my spine at the thought. After a few more minutes of breathing, I exit the bathroom to find everyone waiting for me. Except Matthew, of course, who is out like a light.

"Are you ready, Princess?" Adrian asks, holding his hand out. I suck in a grounding breath, and then I take it.

CHAPTER TWENTY
LIAM

Contrary to what movies and television may portray, the meeting with the queen is not in a grand throne room lined with gold filigree. Adrian, Dylan, and I follow Serenity and a member of the royal guard to the queen's grand study, which is, actually, lined with gold filigree. An elegant chair sits in the round nook that contains towering windows, and an entire wall is taken up by a mahogany bookshelf. The walls are the same stone of the rest of the ancient palace, and a fire roars in the hearth.

The queen stands from one of the plush armchairs, a book clenched in her grasp. It doesn't appear that she'd been reading it, though. As she faces us, I kneel, along with the rest of the men. Serenity is the only one left standing, and she twists her hands in front of us and watches us with uncertainty.

"May I introduce Queen Amelie Adelaide Violette," the guard says, his voice far too loud in the silence of the smallish room.

Serenity seems to come to, giving an awkward and clumsy little curtsy. Her mind is a jumble of thoughts, but the main one is how young the queen appears.

"You may stand," Queen Amelie says, her voice lyrical. I straighten and approach Serenity, resting a hand on her lower back. The queen's eyes dart to me, and I have to work to not shrink under her gaze.

"I expected you to be wearing a ballgown," Serenity says, a hushed laugh catching in her throat. I smile, and the queen responds with a resounding laugh. She's wearing a pair of tailored navy slacks and a ruffled white blouse under a tan blazer. Her feet are in a pair of heels that make her nearly as tall as Dylan.

"Only on special occasions," Amelie replies, approaching Serenity carefully. Can Serenity see the nerves in her mother's eyes? The fear? The tiny spark of hope?

Serenity stands stark still as the queen reaches out, resting her palm on her cheek. At that, she sucks in a breath, and tears well in the ruler's eyes. This show of emotion is unprecedented. In all my years in the palace, I have never seen Amelie cry.

"Sérénité," she says, her accented voice thick with emotion. Serenity shivers, and the queen pulls her into her arms. "I feared I may never see you again. And you look so much like me."

Serenity slowly returns the hug, and I have to look away from the emotion blooming on her face. Her thoughts have stalled, and I have to forcefully remove myself from her mind.

SERENITY

*M*om.

Growing up, I've never understood the bond my friends and classmates have felt for their mothers. Not when mine was cold and unforgiving.

Now, though, as I'm enveloped in a warm hug

from this woman I've just met, I understand.

I breathe in the scent of her, and something breaks open inside of me like a dam giving way to the river's force.

"We will leave you alone," Adrian says from behind me, although I can barely process his words.

When we're alone, she pulls away, taking my face in her hands. I study her features, shocked at the resemblance that I never felt when looking at the mother I grew up with. Her eyebrows arch the same as mine, and her lips are just a little uneven, fuller on the bottom than the top.

"I can't believe it's really you," she says with a breathy laugh. A finger traces down my nose, and her eyes crinkle. "And you have Tomas's nose."

I tilt my head. "I have a father?"

The queen—my mother—smiles and nods. "You have three, although it's clear now that you're grown who your biological father is."

I don't know what to do with this information. My dad's missed calls burn in the back of my mind. My mom might have been awful to me growing up, but he'd always been kind. If it hadn't been for him, I wouldn't have made it through.

Still, a tiny voice in my head reminds me that

he never did anything to stop her cruelty.

"We can discuss all that later, though," she says, pulling away from me. The loss of her warmth sends a pang through my heart. Something in my soul knows, without a doubt, that this woman is my mother. That something draws me to her, and being with her now is like taking a deep breath after being underwater for years. "For now, I want to know about you. I missed everything, and I don't think I can stand the feeling of not knowing you any longer." She sits on the loveseat in front of the fire, then pats the cushion beside her.

I sit down, trying to look prim and proper like her. "I'm not really sure what to tell you," I admit. "I grew up in New York with my mom and dad and brother." I shrug. "Not a lot to tell."

Her eyes brighten with interest, and she leans forward. "New York? That's so far from where we sent you."

I nod. "Yeah, well I didn't even know I was adopted until Adrian found me. I mean, a few minutes before."

She nods. "I understand. This must be a difficult time for you."

I sigh. "I mean, I guess I haven't really thought about it all that much. Between almost dying several times and the whole dragon thing, it's been a lot."

"Almost dying?" she asks. Her accent is the same as Adrian's, which I've come to realize is a Draecus accent. I would rather not talk about my life. There's so much more that I would like to know about dragons that I don't understand.

I shrug. "Yeah." I can almost feel the gag being shoved in my mouth, the rope around my neck, the racing of my heart and the scream I couldn't get out.

Amelie shakes her head, then puts a hand on my knee. "It's alright. You don't have to speak of such things. If you'd like, I can set you an appointment with the palace psychiatrist."

I shake my head. I wouldn't even know what to say to a psychiatrist. "It's alright. Maybe later." I don't plan on seeing this person, though. I don't need therapy, I need an explanation. Or maybe a nap. Or something to eat. "Honestly, I'm just tired. And a bit stressed. Like you said, it's been a long day."

Her eyebrows scrunch together, and guilt floods through me. She'd been so excited to talk to me, and I've barely said more than a few words to her. "I understand. I will have dinner brought to your room."

"I have a room?" I ask.

She nods. "Of course. I had it prepared when Adrian and his team began searching for you."

I can handle a lot, but the fact that I already have my own room in this huge palace tips me over the edge. I suck in a deep breath, clenching my hands on the fine fabric of my overpriced skirt.

The room seems to shrink around me, and all sound goes fuzzy. The queen is trying to speak with me, but her words won't come through. I clench my teeth as my muscles become sore, and she rests a hand on my cheek.

"You will not transform here," she says, her voice a command that breaks through the noise. Suddenly, everything is normal again. I can breathe, and my body feels fine.

"How did you do that?" I breathe, unable to keep my eyes away from hers.

"That is my power," she says with a frown. "I rarely use it, but I can bind dragons with my word."

A shiver runs through me at the intense look on her face. The idea that she could tell anyone to do anything at all has terrifying implications. I set my jaw and nod.

"I do not take this power lightly," she says, releasing her hold on me. "I only use it when absolutely necessary. And I believe that your powers may reveal themselves soon."

I shake my head. I know what my power is. My hands catch fire and ruin my life. Honestly, anything else is too much for me to handle.

"I want you to begin training immediately," the queen says. Her voice doesn't ring with command, but her tone is non-negotiable. "It is a disservice to you if you don't know what you're doing."

I stand up. "I don't think I can," I say.

Her eyes dart to the door, and she stands to tower over me. Her face is smooth, and I once again wonder how she could be my mother when she doesn't even look a decade older than me. "The rebel groups grow restless. We may have created a treaty with them a quarter of a century ago, but they still believe that dragons should rule over humans. And hunters continue to attack our outer colonies. If you aren't able to control your powers, it will be used against the kingdom. Serenity," she says, using my Americanized name for the first time, "you will need to have strength. I cannot foresee what is coming, but it may just be our downfall without you."

I swallow, but my resolve hardens. "Fine." All I can think of right now are my dragons. Adrian, Liam, Matthew, Dylan. I will do anything for them. And if my mother is convinced that I need to learn to fight, then I will learn to fight.

A guard takes me to my room, and I can't help but gawk at the soft pinks, ivory, and gold filigree. The bed is gigantic and covered in fluffy white blankets and pillows, and the posts look like trees reaching up and holding a delicate ivory canopy. I stare at the murals painted on the ceiling, bronze and pink dragons hurtling through soft clouds.

"Lovely, isn't it?" Adrian asks, and I realize that the guys have been staring at me from the sofas and armchairs by the fireplace, which isn't lit. A chill runs through me despite the heat outside— my room has no windows and is deep within the palace. The guard had explained that it was for safety.

I nod. "It's a lot." I go over and dive into the soft bed, tugging the blankets around me. Matthew, who is still clearly exhausted, joins me.

"How do you feel?" he asks, his voice distant and cold.

"Fine," I lie. Honestly, I'm terrified. I showed up expecting an awkward reunion with the mother I never knew, and now I've been told that I get to fight in a dragon war.

Nobody fights me on the phrase, and they try

to act like nothing's wrong. A young man in a navy blue suit brings us lunch on a cart, and I scarf it down in a very un-princess-like way.

"I guess I'm supposed to start training tomorrow," I explain after taking a swig of water.

Adrian nods, amusement written all over his face. "Yes, and we will be training you. All of us."

I roll my eyes. Fantastic.

Chapter Twenty-One
Serenity

Training is a goddamn nightmare. I've considered myself to be in pretty good shape my whole life. I can run a mile without breaking a sweat, and my deadlift isn't something to turn your head at.

Training for a dragon war, though, is a whole other ballgame.

First thing every morning, I have to get up with Adrian and go to the gym. He has me run on a treadmill for an hour, and if I begin to slow, he reprimands me. I've only seen the kind and caring side of him, and this commanding military version kind of makes me want to kick his ass. I get plenty of chances when we move on to sparring, though, and I can never do more than hit or kick *near* him. I never land a single strike.

Then, I get to sit in a giant library while Liam attempts to teach me the history of the island and our clan. I have so much information stuffed in my head every day that I can't even think by the time I get to my lessons with Dylan, which are my least favorite.

"You need to find your power," Dylan says for what must be the millionth time. Adrian finally seems to trust him around me, and we sit in my room as he explains—badly—how I can access these mysterious powers I'm pretty sure I don't have. He's got the most control over his powers, though, so he's all I've got. While Adrian and Liam and Matthew have incredible powers, Dylan has had to learn to control his out of necessity.

"I don't know what that means," I say, throwing my hands in the air with exasperation.

Dylan seems just as frustrated. A growl takes his throat, and I have to lean back. "I don't know how else to explain it," he says. "It's like…a feeling inside you. Deep inside." He puts a hand on his heart, and I frown.

"Great."

We keep going like this for weeks. No matter how much he explains it or how constipated I probably look from focusing, I simply can't find a magical power inside my brain.

My presence is not made known to most people. Only the queen, her on-island consorts, and my dragons are aware of my identity. To everyone else, I am simply a royal guest, another anonymous dragon who's returned to the island. I like it that way.

The whole time, I don't transform, and I barely see Matthew. He's the only one I've slept with, and now I can barely get him to have a conversation with me.

Every night, someone shares my bed. Adrian is always there, his comforting presence never more than an arm's length away. Sometimes, Dylan or Liam are there as well. One night, it's all three.

No Matthew, though.

One afternoon, as I'm walking down to the kitchen after my lesson with Adrian, I hear a commotion, a raised voice in the hall I'm about to turn into.

I decide to wait around the corner for it to diffuse.

"This is just like you," a man says, his voice

angry and harsh. "You've only ever been useless. If I didn't know better I'd think you really *were* garbage."

I put a hand over my mouth to keep from gasping aloud. What a terrible thing to say to someone! Then, the next voice freezes me in place.

"I'm sorry, father," Matthew says. His voice is blank and emotionless. Every time I've spoken to him, there's been something in his tone, be it anger or desperation or passion. Now, though, there's nothing. It's like he's totally empty.

I take a deep breath and round the corner. Matthew is standing in the middle of the hall, disinterest on his face. A slightly older looking man is standing beside him, although that means he could be hundreds of years old, if my mother's appearance is anything to go by. After I returned to my room, Liam had explained that the queen has been on the throne for nearly three hundred years, which explains why she feels so ageless in behavior but looks so young.

"Matthew," I say warmly. He jerks his head in my direction, and there's a sort of wildness in his eyes that gives me pause.

His father's eyes narrow.

"This must be the human-born you found," he sneers, looking down his nose at me. I swallow a lump that forms in my throat. "Raised by humans and everything." I could correct him, inform him that I'm the goddamn princess of this clan, but I don't want to use that to change his mind.

"And so what if I am?" I ask, holding my head high and keeping the fear out of my voice as best I can. I put my hands on my hips and stare him down. I will not back off.

"You aren't truly one of us," he spits. "You never will be. Not with all that disgusting human blood running through your veins."

Matthew doesn't speak up, and when I meet his eyes, he looks away. Is that shame?

"Your son is human born as well," I point out.

The man laughs. "And what a disappointment he's been." He raises his hand, and Matthew gives the slightest flinch. The man doesn't strike, though, just claps him on the shoulder. "I thought I could train it out of him, but it doesn't seem to have taken."

I grit my teeth. "Well, the only disappointment I see here is you."

The man's face goes red at that, and he looks like he might catch fire. He's a dragon, so it's not entirely unfounded. "Do you know who I am?" he bellows, voice so loud that the whole castle can probably hear him.

"No," I lie. "I don't really care, though." Then, I take Matthew's hand. He doesn't resist, but he doesn't hold my hand back. "Matthew, you should have lunch with me."

I drag him away, and, thankfully, his father doesn't follow. He lets out one last sentence, though, and it chills me to my core. "It would have been better for everyone if you'd died in that dumpster."

My heart races. If it weren't for Matthew's hand in mine, I would turn around and punch that asshole right in the face. He tightens his fingers around mine, though, which gives me the strength to just keep walking.

Instead of continuing on to the kitchen, I lead Matthew down a different route until we reach my room.

"We can have food brought here," I say, pulling him into the bedroom. He doesn't meet my eyes, and when I release him to walk inside, he stays by the door.

"You should come sit," I say, patting the bed beside me as I sit down.

He shakes his head, and the stray hairs that have fallen out of his hair tie brush over his face. "I appreciate the intervention," he says, his voice flat. "But I don't think I should stay."

My heart drops, and I stand back up and walk to him. "Why? Because of your father? You know he's just an asshole, right?"

He looks away so he doesn't have to meet my eyes. I want to know what he's thinking, but he's so closed off. I'm just beginning to realize why he'd been so fierce with me when we first met, and why it took him so long to warm up. All the time it took me to get through his walls had been demolished the instant we showed up here.

"I haven't been given a lot of options in my life, Serenity," he says. Instead of warmth at my name on his lips, I just feel cold. The way he's speaking is scaring me, like I'm talking to a stranger. "It's clear that your mother bound us together when we were young, but..."

I wait, my heart trying to beat out of my chest. Can he not hear what he's doing to me with this conversation?

"I didn't have a choice in the matter. And I think that I should. So even though we're connected, I am choosing for myself."

Nausea rolls through me, and he frowns. He's still not looking at me, though. Instead, his gaze is pinned on the fireplace.

"What are you saying?" I whisper. If I said it any louder, he'd hear the tremble in my tone. I know exactly what he's trying to say, but I have to hear the words. I *deserve* to hear the words.

Finally, he looks at me, his eyes piercing into my heart like a dagger. "I don't want to be with you, Serenity."

And with that, the knife twists, leaving me to bleed out. I don't allow the pain to show on my face. I just nod. If I begged him to stay, it would be selfish of me. No, he should be free to live his life on his own terms. I already have three other men who want to be with me. Demanding more would just be plain wrong.

Still, when he exits the room without another word, I fall to the ground. My heart is shattered, the shards slicing through me and demolishing my insides, and I'm not sure I'll be able to pick up the pieces.

CHAPTER TWENTY-TWO
ADRIAN

I don't leave my room. Adrian tries to get me out, but I can't bring myself to leave my bed for more than a few minutes, and never to go further than the bathroom. He asks me what happened, but I can't put it into words. Liam doesn't leave my side, holding me in his strong arms every night. I fall asleep to the sound of his heart more often than not.

"I brought you food," Dylan says, and I sit up slowly. He sets a tray with a sandwich and an assortment of fruits in front of me. He sits beside me, and I tuck my head into his shoulder so he can hold me.

Adrian stopped asking me what was wrong after day one, which must mean that Liam told him. I'm sure everyone knows that I'm just being pathetic over a boy. I've never been this sad about a relationship ending—in fact, I'm usually the one to end things before they can become too serious. The loss of Matthew, though, is like the loss of a limb.

"Matthew is such a dick," Dylan mumbles, rubbing my arm while I slowly consume a single strawberry.

I shake my head, my heart speeding up marginally. "No, he isn't. I'm just being selfish."

Dylan presses his forehead against the top of my head, and he sighs with clear frustration. "Stop it," he says. "He hurt you, and he's acting like he doesn't even care."

That sends another knife through my heart. This whole time, I'd hoped that he would at least feel sad about leaving me. "He doesn't have to care," I say with a shrug, a tear falling from my eye and soaking into the comforter.

"Serenity, there is no reason for him to be acting this way," Dylan insists. I don't reply to that, so he presses. "We all know he cares about you. He shouldn't be doing this."

I shrug and pull away.

"I'm not really hungry," I say, lying down to face away from him.

Dylan huffs. "Damn it, Serenity. I love you, but you're being impossible."

I hold my breath. His words hang in the air between us. I don't speak for fear of breaking the moment.

The platter is moved, and Dylan joins me under the sheets, wrapping his arms around me. He breathes me in, then, voice low, he says, "I love you, Serenity. I need you to know that."

I let out a shudder. He says that now, but he'll leave me like Matthew did. Like everyone always has.

I curl into myself, and he stays with me, holding me. "I love you," he whispers, over and over again until the words hold no meaning anymore. They're no longer individual words, but a single sound that carries his frustration and hope and something else I can't identify.

No matter how many times he says it, though, I can't bring myself to say it back. Not if it could mean regretting it when he breaks my heart.

CHAPTER TWENTY-THREE
ADRIAN

Matthew is in his room when I find him. It's been three days since he spoke with Serenity, and he's been avoiding me. Avoiding all of us. Well, enough is enough.

I pound on the door.

"Open up, fuckweasel!" I shout. "We need to talk!"

I expect him to ignore me, but after another pound, the door swings open. At first, I barely recognize him. Matthew's usually pristine locks are a mess, wildly sticking out of the greasy bun that looks like it's been there for days.

"What's up, man-bun?" I ask, shoving my way

inside. Matthew has never once worn his hair like that, and his clothes are a pair of sweatpants with some sort of food or drink stains on them.

"Leave me alone," he says, going back to his bed. I kick a pair of boxers that are strewn along with a bunch of other clothes, and I notice some sort of smashed porcelain on the floor beneath a new dent in the drywall.

"You're being an ass," I say, crossing my arms over my chest. "I mean, you've always been a bit of an ass, but right now you're being a super ass."

Matthew tosses an arm over his eyes. "Seriously, it's none of your business."

I let out a humorless laugh. "None of my business? My best friend looks like shit. Serenity hasn't left her room in three days. She's basically catatonic. I think this is more my business than a lot of shit you've done."

He freezes when I say her name, but he doesn't say anything about her. "I'm not talking about this with you."

I run a hand through my hair. I could really kick his ass right about now, but there's no way it would be a fair fight. Not with the pathetic condition he's in.

"Well, too bad. Because I'm not leaving until you do. Is this about your dad?" I demand.

Matthew is usually a reasonable guy, but being around his father always seems to turn him irrational.

"No," Matthew says, his voice strained.

I must have hit a nerve. Instead of steering away, though, I poke at it.

"I guess he's right," I say casually. "Because if you're gonna be so stubborn that you can't even talk to her, then you are a coward."

Matthew leaps out of bed and storms over to me, jabbing me in the chest with a finger. "You have no idea what you're talking about."

He glances to the closed door behind me, just a flicker, but it's enough to give me pause.

"Matthew," I say. "What is going on?"

He turns around and tries to run his fingers through his ratty hair, but he ends up yanking the ponytail holder out in frustration. The rubber snaps and flies across the room.

"I can't..." he starts. "I don't..." A frustrated sound comes out of him, and he spins back to me, his eyes suddenly feral.

"He'll destroy her," he finally says. "When he finds out who she is, if he finds out about us..." He stops talking, looks at the door, then looks at me. Suddenly, his voice is so quiet that I have to lean toward him. "She wouldn't be safe, Adrian.

I can't keep her safe unless I stay away."

Before I can ask anything else, Matthew jerks the door open, shoves me out, and slams it in my face.

His words have left me with more questions than answers. I pace the hall in front of his door, but it's pretty clear he's done talking.

I leave the hall, climbing up one set of stairs and descending another until I reach the wing of the palace where all the politics happen. Phillip, the queen's third mate, exits a room just as I round a corner, and I jog up to catch him. I didn't even know he'd returned.

"Phillip," I say, taking his arm.

He turns to me, pleasant surprise written on his face. "Adrian," he says. "I'm surprised to see you here."

I release him. "I need an audience with the queen. It's an emergency."

His face goes serious in an instant. "Of course." Phillip has always trusted me. As my mentor growing up, he's been like a second father.

He leads me to her study, then tells me to wait inside.

I pace anxiously, trying my best to not freak out. What had Matthew meant about protecting Serenity from his father? His father is an asshole, but he would never harm a member of the royal family. Does Matthew think he'd try to use her as a pawn?

As my thoughts begin to spiral out of control, the door opens behind me. I spin to find Queen Amelie standing there, and I drop to a knee instantly.

"My lady," I say.

"Stand," she says. "Phillip told me it was urgent."

I do as she says and nod curtly. "It is. As you may know, Serenity hasn't been attending her lessons, and she hasn't been eating."

The queen's jaw goes tight, and worry floats in her eyes. "Correct."

"Matthew told her that he didn't want her. And I think you know why that's suspicious."

A whoosh of air leaves the queen, and she looks almost defeated. "So you figured it out."

I have to keep from rolling my eyes. It had been pretty obvious to all of us within a few days of knowing Serenity that there was something more to the story than we knew.

"Yes," she admits. "I bound you all together that night. I knew you were all human-born children, and I used that to attempt to protect my daughter."

"I know," I say, growing impatient. "But that's not what this meeting is about. I think there might be a danger to the crown."

Amelie's eyes narrow. "And what makes you think that?"

I tell her what Matthew said, then explain my suspicions about his father.

"I know it's not much to go on," I admit, "but I have a feeling about this."

Amelie sits in one of the leather armchairs, tapping her fingers on her knee in thought.

"Well, I cannot confront him," she says slowly as a plan seems to form in her mind. "But we may be able to draw him out, along with any other rebels stirring up dissent."

Her resolve hardens, and she looks at me, her eyes so much like Serenity's that it leaves me breathless.

"I think it is time that we announce the return of our princess," she says.

CHAPTER TWENTY-FOUR
SERENITY

"A debut ball?" I ask. It's the first time I've left my room all week, and my mother has just proposed the most insane idea ever to me.

Henri and Tomas sit beside her, and I try to not look at them. I still haven't had a real chance to speak with either of them, although I can see the resemblance to me in Tomas's features. Adrian told me that Phillip has returned, but I haven't even met this mysterious third man yet.

"I think it's time the world knew about you," Amelie says. "There is a lot to prepare, but we will be throwing it in two weeks, so I'd like for you to begin preparations. You will be fit for a gown and officially crowned as the princess of the Draecus Clan."

Adrian had also filled me in on what Matthew said, although I'm not sure I believe him when he claims that Matthew definitely wants to be with me.

"And you think this will draw out any sort of rebellion?" I ask.

It doesn't seem like the best plan. In fact, I'm a bit concerned about the possibility of being killed by rebel assassins at the party.

"Don't worry," Henri interjects. "We will have the best security in the world. You will never be in harm's way, but we believe that a public debut will be the best way to draw out any hidden rebels."

I nod. I'm still not totally convinced, but they all seem fairly certain that this is going to happen no matter what objections I may have about it.

I try to avoid looking at the two men sitting on either side of the queen—my mother, I correct myself for the millionth time—but it's hard not to glance at them occasionally, wondering what my childhood may have been like had they raised me. Despite our limited interaction, my heart warms every time Henri passes me the rolls that I devour at dinner or Tomas brings me my favorite flavor of gatorade while I'm training with Adrian.

"How would this even work?" I ask, sitting on my hands to keep from fidgeting like a kid. "I mean, I know how to dance, but who would I dance with? What am I supposed to say to people?"

My mother leans forward and rests a hand on my knee. "Don't worry," she says with a smile. "We will take care of everything. And as for dancing, I assumed you would dance with your mates."

Heat floods my face, and I have to cough as I choke on a bit of saliva that I sucked down the wrong tube.

"Mates?" I gasp out.

She sits back. "Why, yes. Unless you are not comfortable making the official announcement?"

I shake my head, my wavy, sun-brightened hair falling across my face like a privacy curtain. "I just..." Matthew crosses my mind. He'd been pretty clear that he wants to stay away from me from now on. A lump forms in my throat, but I swallow it down. I will not cry now. At the very least, I can wait until I return to my room. Why should I even be sad? It's not like being unwanted is new to me.

A little voice in the back of my head tells me that maybe the sex had just been that bad, but I shake it away. I don't have time to entertain such thoughts, although the fact that I haven't actually gone any further with the rest of the guys proves that it's something I've thought about before, even if it's not in the very front of my mind.

"I think I might wait to…announce anything," I say, trying to speak past the mounting embarrassment and anxiety that tie my stomach in knots and block my vocal cords.

She nods. "Alright. Well, we haven't time to waste. My seamstress will be waiting in your suite to go over designs and take your measurements.

I am rushed out of the room and led back up to my suite in a haze. I have to choose between what feels like hundreds of fabric swatches, but the seamstress seems satisfied with my choice. Then, I stand in silence while she measures me for what I'm sure will be an awe-worthy gown worth more than anything I've ever owned combined.

Fighting lessons are put on hold as I prepare for the ball. As it turns out, my obligatory dance lessons from childhood were not nearly enough for a royal event, so I have to practice with an instructor half the day while the other half is spent learning the names and faces of all the members of the royal court.

I barely get a moment to myself, and even less time with Adrian, Liam, or Dylan. I don't ask them about Matthew, and every time I think I catch a glance of him in the halls of the palace, he disappears like a phantom. My heart still aches for him, but I know there's nothing to be done. I keep my chin up and walk with purpose, a stance that would make my overbearing adoptive mother proud. Either that, or she'd pick something else to despise about me. Probably the latter.

I still haven't contacted my friends or family, but everyone here seems to think that's for the best. At night, though, lying in bed and thinking about my past, I wonder what they all think. That I ran away when I found out about my adoption? Or that I'm dead at the bottom of the Hudson River? That seems more likely.

"What are you thinking about?" Adrian asks, brushing my hair away from my face as we lie in the dark.

I shake my head, my eyes drifting shut as the week's events overtake me. "Just worrying," I mumble.

He chuckles, but there's concern in his tone when he replies, "I can tell. You know you can talk to me about anything, right?"

I nod, then realize he probably can't see me in the pitch-dark room. "I know. It's just a lot of nonsense, really." I don't want to admit that I can't stop thinking about Matthew and about my old life, both things I will never get back. I don't want to tell Adrian that. Not about Matthew, because I don't want to seem ungrateful for the affection Adrian gives me, and not about my past life, because Adrian is the one who took me away from it all. No, it's best to just not tell him. "I hope I don't make a fool of myself."

This isn't technically a lie. Although I finally believe that I'm a dragon, and a dragon princess at that, I still don't think I'm anywhere near qualified enough to take on what's expected of me. I've never been good enough for the woman I thought to be my mother, the woman who was supposed to love me. How could I possibly be good enough to be a princess?

Adrian's hand rubs down my arm, and a shiver runs down my body, goosebumps rising on my skin at his touch.

"You'll do amazing," he says. "It's just a few hours in two days, and then we'll have time to be together. All you need to do is get through one night, and I promise it will be fine."

I have to believe that's true. If I can just get through the weekend, everything will work out.

CHAPTER TWENTY-FIVE
SERENITY

The day of the ball arrives far too quickly. Yesterday was my final dress fitting, and it had felt like a second skin on me, the fabric softer than a baby bunny's fur. The back has a zipper instead of buttons, by my request since I'm sick of buttoning up all the fancy clothes that fill the closet of my suite. Now, the gown is zipped in a garment bag and hanging on the outside of my wardrobe.

I don't see anyone I know all day, other than the seamstress who's been a silent companion for the past two weeks. My hair is put in a low bun that is far more voluminous than I thought a bun could be, and little ringlets fall to frame my face. A liberal amount of hairspray is put in, and then a third person I've never met approaches my face with all sorts of makeup tools that I'm not used to using. I usually just do a dab of mascara, but this guy is touching my face for what must be hours, and that's after an hour or more of hair work.

"I adore your nose," the man, Hans, says, brushing something on my cheeks while he holds my chin up with one finger. I learned very quickly that he wasn't afraid to grab my face to move it as needed, so I comply with every motion. I don't think he means to be so pushy, but it's clear he wants to finish this.

"Thanks," I say slowly. I've never really thought of my long, slightly arched nose as something to love, just a part of my face that does its job. "It lets me breathe?"

The man chuckles, his minty breath pushing through my hair like a breeze.

"So are you a dragon?" I ask, doing my best to not move my mouth too much. He's already gotten onto me once for talking.

He shakes his head. "Oh, no. I'm just one of the imported palace artisans. I've been in the fashion industry for years, but I had no idea dragons existed until I married one."

I raise my eyebrows, and he frowns. I put them back down. "Oh?"

He nods. "Yes. I love my husband, but his world gets complicated."

That brings even more questions to my mind.

"So it's just the two of you?" I haven't spent time with many other dragons, but aside from the four—no, three—men who surround me, I've seen my mother with two of her three spouses. *Mates,* I think, testing the word in my head.

He nods. "Yes. He was never one for the dragonesses, if you can understand that."

I roll my eyes, just about the only motion I can do without a stern look from him. "Dude, I'm from New York. Ninety percent of the population up there is gay or otherwise."

He nods, and a light, wistful smile crosses his face. "Ah, Fashion Week. How I miss it sometimes. If it weren't for all the damn hunters, Antonio and I would probably return. As it is, though, it's far too dangerous."

That sobers up the light mood I'd been trying to implement. I can almost feel the hunter's gag in my mouth, and I almost cry with relief when Hans pulls away from me. "Done," he says, his face lighting up as the somber thoughts seem to flee his mind. I only wish it were that simple for me.

He turns me to face the mirror, and I gasp. Why have I never had professional makeup applied?

Instead of my short, nearly translucent lashes, I have a pair of fake lashes that nearly brush my brows, and the pale lip stain is subtle. My face is contoured in a way I've never been able to accomplish, and my once hidden cheekbones are obvious now, sharp enough to cut glass. Somehow, though, it almost looks like I'm not wearing any makeup. If I didn't know better, I'd think I was looking at a naturally stunning stranger. Is this how models and movie stars manage to look so incredible all the time?

"Wow," I breathe, and Hans makes a grunt of pleasure.

"This is why they hire me," he says, packing up the makeup suitcase he brought to my room with him.

He leaves, and, for the first time all day, I'm alone. I want to reach up to touch my face, but I'm terrified of ruining the work of art he's created.

Suddenly, like it's been waiting for me to be by myself, the terror of what we're about to do sets in. I am the lost princess of Draecus Island. I am a dragon. Like an actual dragon with scales and wings and fire powers.

And there are people who want to kill me.

I am about to go out to announce to the world that I'm the best target for dragon haters.

Before I can fall too deeply into this spiral, someone knocks softly on the door, so quiet that I almost don't hear it.

"Serenity?" Liam says, opening the door a crack.

I spin around, crossing my arms over my chest even though I'm wearing a robe that covers my beige underwear—all custom-made for this event, of course.

He rushes in when he sees the look on my face, and it's clear he's been listening to my thoughts as worry takes over. Instead of being in a pair of jeans and a t-shirt, though, he's wearing a tuxedo, the jacket a forest green velvet with black silk lapels. "It'll be alright," he promises. *Just like Matthew had,* my traitorous mind says. He wraps me in his arms, and the worries melt away. Then, I finally come back to myself and jerk out of his arms.

"My makeup!" His jacket doesn't even have the slightest smudge on it, though, and when I check myself in the mirror, there's not even the tiniest flaw in Hans's work. Even my hair is still perfect.

When I turn back to Liam, though, I notice a young woman standing behind him.

"Um," I say, giving Liam a pointed look. He startles and turns to her.

"Ah, yes. Serenity, this is Gwen. She's one of the palace maids, and she's here to help you into your shoes and gown."

I'd assumed I would just change myself, but it's a bit of a relief knowing that there will be someone else to help me. What if I were to ruin my gown before even making it to the ball?

The girl gives a little curtsy, which makes me feel incredibly awkward. Should I do it back? I look to Liam for help, and he gives the tiniest shake of his head. Thank goodness he's here.

"I'll see you out there," Liam says, leaning down and giving the most chaste kiss possible to my cheek. Before I even have the chance to ask him to stay, he's gone.

"Nice to meet you," I saw awkwardly to Gwen.

A tense smile comes across her face. "You as well," she says. Then, she rushes over to the wardrobe and pulls down the garment back, taking it over to lay on my bed before unzipping it. A nearly inaudible gasp escapes her, and I catch her stroking the fabric.

"It's lovely," she breathes, then glances up to me.

"Thank you."

Without much preamble, she pulls out the dress, then helps me into it after I remove my robe. She has to put it over my head like I'm a kid, and then the delicate zipper goes smoothly up my back and to the back of my neck, where only lace covers my skin instead of the built-in slip that goes from my bust to my knees. The rose gold flower pattern hugs the curves I didn't even know I had, the flowers glinting gently in the golden light of the room, and the skirt flares out just above the knees, layers and layers of translucent silk below. The train is a bit long, but not so much that I'll trip over the front in my high heels, which Gwen helps me step into next.

"Lovely," she says, a tight smile on her face.

"I can't imagine that it's much fun working these kind of events," I say, my face falling into a frown.

She shrugs. "It pays well, so I don't mind."

I want to argue with her, but the clock in my room chimes delicately as seven o'clock comes around.

I'm late.

"You'd best be going," she says, then her eyes dart to the door. She bites her lip, suddenly looking worried.

"What's wrong?" I ask. I shouldn't pry into her life, as it's none of my business, but she sort of looks like a deer who's about to get hit by a car.

As another knock sounds at the door, she grabs my arm, scrunching the translucent lace that goes to my wrists.

"I know something horrible about one of the men you came with," she whispers, fear evident in her voice. I'm about to tell her that Dylan won't hurt me, but the name she utters instead stops me in my tracks. "Matthew Delecroix."

"Serenity?" Tomas's voice calls from the other side of the door.

"Just a moment," I call back, my voice far too high. This is the first time anyone other than Dylan has spoken his name aloud since the incident. I have to know what she has to say.

"You cannot trust him. It may be none of my business, but I've heard things. Nobody pays mind to servants, not even those who plot against the crown."

I open my mouth to speak, but what can I say? It's not like I can defend him. If I'm being honest with myself, I don't actually know him. Had the whole thing on the boat been to get close to me? If that's the case, though, why would he then abandon me the moment we reached the island?

"Do not trust him," she hisses. "He will only betray you."

Tomas knocks again, and Gwen releases my arm.

I have to steady my shaking hands, and then I go to the door, opening it to reveal Henri and Tomas. Another man that I recognize as Phillip stands behind them, his expression awkward and uncomfortable. After this is all over, it would be nice to actually introduce myself to him.

What am I supposed to do with this new information?

CHAPTER TWENTY-SIX
SERENITY

My heart pounds in my chest as I try to process the events of the evening, but I am swept up so quickly that I don't know where to focus.

After leaving my room, Henri and Tomas each loop an arm through mine, escorting me on either side. We follow Phillip through the halls, down toward the ballroom. I should feel like a princess, but instead I feel like a prisoner being sent to my death.

He will only betray you.

I'm tempted to ask Tomas and Henri about it,

but I really don't know them well enough to confide these feelings.

"It's all going to be fine," Henri mumbles, patting my arm gently with his free hand. I take in a deep breath, then blow it out slowly through my nose. I will not cause a scene. After the party, I'll speak with Adrian.

Instead of the usual electric overhead lighting, the halls are lined with sconces that hold torches. In the flickering light, I almost feel like I'm in a medieval palace. In this light, the tapestries that line the walls come alive, the subtle metal strands in them glinting from the flame, almost giving the appearance of movement.

"Breathe, Serenity," Tomas says as we approach the final door, the one that leads to the steps into the palace ballroom. There is a low murmur of sound from the other side, the conversations muffled from the door.

Faintly, a voice calls out above all the rest, "I am pleased to announce that, after years away from us, our Princess has returned." Queen Amelie's voice is powerful and commanding, but not in the magical way it had been before. This is just her. In this moment, I'm proud to be her daughter. "May I introduce my daughter, Princess Sérénité Amalia Claudette."

At that moment, the doors ahead of us open, and, just like we've practiced all week, Henri and Tomas lead me forward. The room had been grand before, but now it's something out of a fairytale. The walls are pale ivory lined with gold filigree, and it glistens in the hundreds—if not thousands—of candles that line the room. Ahead of me is an ornate balcony, and to either side are two curved staircases that lead down to the glittering marble floor.

My mother is standing at the balcony, and she lifts a hand for me to take. I take in a grounding breath and step forward out of Henri and Tomas' grasps, taking her hand. Her face is warm and so filled with love that it sends a shock of pain through my heart. Her hand is warm and reassuring, and I smile tentatively. As long as I don't look down at the crowd of people below, I'll be fine. We've rehearsed this a dozen times. A roar of applause deafens me, and I keep the smile on my face, unfocusing my eyes so the people below just look like a big blur.

We split apart, each of us walking down a separate staircase. Somehow, Henri is already prepared to take the queen's hand on her side. I'm not even sure how he got down there so fast. At the base of my staircase to greet me is Adrian, the one man that everyone knows I'm bound to. Dylan and Liam are somewhere in the crowd, and my eyes search for them.

"You're doing great," Adrian mumbles into my hair. I loop my hand through his extended arm, and he leads me through the crowd to the head of the room. The crowd parts, a blur of smiling faces passing as I focus on not falling in front of all these people. Adrian's strong arm is steady, and I remember that he would never let me fall.

After what feels like a mile-long walk, we reach the platform that holds four intricate chairs, the one in the center more ornate and plush than the rest.

My mother and I meet into the center, our escorts dropping our arms. Gwen appears from behind the thrones, and the sight of her is like a shock to my system. What else does she know?

Those who would destroy the crown.

She doesn't look at me or my mother, her eyes low as she carries a wooden box with inlaid mother of pearl. The warm lighting in the room suddenly feels ominous rather than magical, and I can't help but glance out to the crowd in search of any sign of any sort of danger. Instead, I find Matthew.

His eyes are dark, but steady on me. He towers

over the men standing near him, so he definitely stands out in his tux with the velvet maroon blazer and black lapels. His hair is braided along the sides, and the top is in a loose braid that gives him some volume. With a start, I realize that he has the exact same hair he did the day we…

I shake that thought out of my head. The only difference in his hair now is the silver beadwork woven in. My heart reaches out to him without my permission, but his face is unreadable. He's just here out of obligation.

My mother takes my hand, and I turn my face to her. There must be something in my expression, because hers falters for the smallest fraction of a second. Still, she opens the box Gwen carries, and I gasp.

I'd been told I would be receiving a crown at the ball, but this is not what I'd been expecting. It is a delicate gold that wraps in a full circle, coming up to several matching points all the way around. When I look closer, though, the gold looks like vines that weave through each other, little leaves and flowers sprouting from them. Throughout the vines are inlaid diamonds and rose quartz, as well as pale pink freshwater pearls.

I kneel, just like I've been practicing. I keep my eyes on the floor, although they desperately want to dart back over to Matthew. The queen places the crown on my head, and it's shockingly heavy for something so delicate. As she tells me to stand, I can't help but look to where Matthew was standing.

He's gone, and the crowd erupts into applause and cheers.

Before the queen can utter another word, though, a boom shakes the ground.

My eyes meet hers, and her expression is filled with a fear I'd never imagined could come from such a powerful woman. Then, her face hardens. "Everyone, we ask that you remain calm. This palace is fortified against any attacks." She snaps her head to the side. "Adrian, take the princess to her quarters. Keep her safe."

Adrian quickly takes my hand and rushes me away, and I kick off my heels to keep up.

"What's going on?" I demand, but he doesn't answer. My heart pounds so hard it feels like it's in my throat. "Where are Liam and Dylan?" *And Matthew,* I don't add.

"They're fine," he says.

That's not an answer, but I don't tell him that. As we round the corner just before my room, I spot a figure standing stock still. He's wearing a maroon jacket, and his hair is down in braids.

"Matthew," Adrian says with a sigh of relief. "Take Serenity. Don't let anyone in the room."

Before I can protest, Adrian shuffles me past the door and leans down for a rough kiss.

"I love you, Princess," he says breathlessly. Why does it sound like he's leaving me?

Before I can respond, he closes my door, leaving me locked in the room with Matthew.

He will only betray you.

"Serenity," he says, his voice as dark as his expression. A muscle in his jaw ticks as he approaches me.

"Stay back," I gasp, backing against the door. There's nowhere for me to go. If Gwen is right, then Matthew could be the key to my destruction.

He ignores me, putting a finger under my chin and lifting my face. His eyes bore into mine, and I gasp. Before I can do anything, though, his lips close over mine.

CHAPTER TWENTY SEVEN
MATTHEW

The past few weeks have been hell. Every thought in my head, every emotion I've felt have all been about Serenity. She's like a drug I didn't know I was addicted to until I went without her.

With my lips on hers, it's like I can finally breathe again. The fear that had been in her expression evaporates as her body relaxes against mine, and I wrap my arms around her waist to hold her against me.

Slowly, like she's coming back to herself, she wraps her arms around my neck, her fingers winding through my hair.

"God, Serenity," I groan, moving down to kiss her cheek, her jaw, her neck. As she tilts her head back, her gold crown clinks against the door, and her body stiffens once again.

"No," she shouts, shoving me away. I stumble back, my arms suddenly empty. I want nothing more than to pull her back into my embrace, but she wraps her arms around herself, reaching up to touch her lips with her fingertips.

"Serenity, I'm sorry," I say. My voice is hoarse. I haven't spoken to anyone in a while, refusing to allow even Adrian near me since the conversation we had before. I thought I was strong enough to stay away from her, but the attack on the castle sprung me into action. The queen sounded confident about the palace's sturdiness, but I realized that people die during this type of thing. If there's even the slightest possibility of my death, I refuse to let it be without the one thing I want most in the world.

I will not die with Serenity thinking I hate her.

Someone pounds on the door, and I reach out and grab Serenity, dragging her behind me on instinct alone. My hands warm with the fire inside, but I don't call out.

"Serenity," someone calls. I don't quite recognize the voice, but it's male. She tries to go around me, but I hold her back.

"No," I command.

She looks up at me, and I can feel her heart racing, smell the fear in her blood.

"It's not safe," I whisper. The only ones that I will allow in this room are Adrian, Liam, and Dylan. In this moment, nobody else can be trusted.

"Serenity, I've been sent by your mother." Then, the voice clicks. It's one of the queen's personal guards. Slowly, I approach the door.

"She asked me to protect you," he says, and the doorknob rattles.

If he's one of the queen's guards, then he may know more about the situation at hand. I hold my hand out to Serenity so she doesn't come any closer, and I crack the door open.

"Mr. Delacroix," he says, his face turning surprised. "I was not expecting you."

I nod tersely, then open the door a bit wider. Before he can step in, though, his face falls.

"What's going on?" I ask, my brain slow to catch up with what is before my eyes. When I look down, a sword is protruding from the man's chest. I stumble back and move to slam the door, but it's too late. A foot blocks the door from closing, and my eyes focus on the man in front of me.

"Father," I say, watching him toss the guard's body to the side like it's garbage.

He frowns with disdain. There are others with him, obscured in the shadows of the hall. All of the sconces have been put out, but I count at least four people hiding from view. "Matthew," he says, his voice as cold and cruel as ever. "What a disappointment you've always been."

My hands are frozen on the door, and my breath is caught in my throat. My brain is tripping over itself.

My father killed a guard.

My father has a group of men with him.

My father is at Serenity's room.

The queen expected rebels to attack Serenity at the ball.

Before I can move to keep him away, the sword plunges forward. I don't even have time to block it.

Serenity screams. I want to tell her that it's okay, that everything is going to be alright. It missed me, obviously. Otherwise I would feel it.

Right?

My head turns down, and the sight that meets me makes no sense.

There is a sword in my chest. Right between

the third and fourth rib.

I don't understand.

He tugs the weapon away, and I turn to face Serenity. My vision blurs, and my head spins. *I'm okay*, I want to say. *Don't worry about me. Run.*

Instead, I fall to the ground.

CHAPTER TWENTY-EIGHT
SERENITY

*M*atthew is dead.

The thought doesn't process. It can't be true. Only a moment ago, he'd been kissing me like we were the only people alive.

Dead.

He lies on the ground, blood seeping through his jacket and spreading across the marble floor. The splash of red against white is so shocking that it's almost cartoonish. Nothing in the world is that red, right?

I feel the shift coming on, my body rolling with anger and shock and sadness that I can't quite process.

You will not shift here.

My mother's command strikes me like a slap, and I can't move.

Is it possible that she hadn't been specific enough? That instead of keeping me from shifting that day in her study, she'd kept me from shifting at all?

I try to find the dragoness inside, but the shift has abandoned me as quickly as it came.

I take a step toward Matthew, my bare foot landing in a puddle of his blood.

His eyes are open. Why are they open? Shouldn't he at least blink? I kneel, the blood soaking into the gown that had taken weeks to make. I reach for his face, brushing his mess of hair away. It falls, growing damp with blood just like my dress.

Something in me breaks. Something I hadn't even known was there, a wall deep inside that crumbles like it's been hit by an earthquake. My skin buzzes like I've been struck by lightning.

"Serenity, you need to come with us."

The words don't make sense. Matthew can't speak. He's dead.

He's dead he's dead he's dead Matthew is dead.

A hand lands on my shoulder, and I reach up to touch it, smearing blood that had been on the ground. My other hand remains on Matthew's cheek.

I don't recognize the rough hand in mine, and I glance up, my head moving slower than I mean it to. The man is familiar somehow.

Matthew's father, my brain supplies.

A sword is in his hand, dripping with blood.

Matthew's blood.

"You killed him," I whisper.

The man's jaw clenches, and I tighten my hand on his. His face goes pale, and the lightning in me turns into an inferno, radiating from the spot where my hand touches his. It roars through me like a wildfire, destroying everything in its path.

He tries to jerk away from me like I've burned him, but my hand is a vice around his. My body is immovable stone. The flames inside turn everything black, and I turn to face Matthew, ignoring the struggling man desperately trying to escape.

"I should have protected you," I say, leaning forward and pressing my lips to his forehead.

At that moment, the fire goes out. I try to hold on, but I'm already too far from myself. It's like I'm trapped on an island in my mind, and the

shore is too far to swim in shark-infested waters.
It's easier to let go.

CHAPTER TWENTY-NINE
ADRIAN

The sound of Serenity's scream is what alerts me. The queen gives me a nod, and I abandon my post. I weave through the castle hallways, and it's like a dream that makes running too slow and hallways too long. My mind races, trying to imagine what may have happened to make her scream that way.

By the time I reach her bedroom, though, she isn't there.

The side in front of me sends shockwaves through my system, and, for the first time since I was a child, I have to force myself to not transform. *Not here.*

Not in front of Matthew's bloodied form on the floor.

Liam runs in from the other side of the hallway, and he freezes when he sees where my gaze is.

"Shit," he mutters.

I have to step over the guard that Amelie had sent, walking slowly toward my friend.

We grew up together.

We would run through the castle corridors, spar in the courtyard with our trainers, learn to shift, hold each other when the other cried over the pain.

He's a grown man, but right now, he looks small, like the kid I grew up with.

Dragons can live for centuries. Millenia, even.

He was only twenty-nine years old.

Another body lies on the floor beside him with no obvious injuries, but his face is pale with death. Well, at least one good thing came out of this. Matthew's father is dead.

I lean over him, ready to at least close his eyes when a ragged gasp drags through his body.

"That's not possible," Liam says, placing a hand on my shoulder like he's going to drag me away.

Another breath runs through Matthew's body,

though, and he struggles to sit up. That's the moment when my training finally comes through, and I press his shoulder down.

"Don't move," I say. Tears of fear or relief or both fall from my eyes, and I unbutton his jacket and then his shirt. There's a hole in his clothing from a sword, probably the one lying on the floor by his father, but there is no injury.

"What the fuck?" Liam asks, leaning over the both of us.

"Serenity," Matthew says, his voice gravelly and choked. He turns and coughs, and blood spits out of his mouth at the hacking.

But he isn't bleeding.

"Where is she?" Matthew asks between coughs. He uses my shoulder to heave himself into a sitting position.

I hadn't been seeing things, though.

A moment ago, Matthew had been dead. His aura had been gone.

Now, though, it's coming back. It's slow, but it's definitely there.

"Adrian," Matthew demands, grabbing my jaw with a hand once he's sitting. "Where. Is. Serenity."

I glance around. She's not in the room. There's no sign of a struggle, though. She must be somewhere, right? I close my eyes and reach out for her aura, but I can't feel it. The connection I feel to her is still there, though. It keeps my heart beating, and I would know in an instant if it was broken.

"She's gone," Liam answers, holding his hand out. Matthew grasps his forearm and hauls himself up. I stand slower, then look to his dead father, who doesn't have the same miraculous recovery.

"Matthew," I say, the words finally coming to me. "You were dead."

Matthew makes heavy eye contact with me, then looks down to his father's corpse, the life drained out of him. Looking at his body now, it's like he's been dead for weeks. Months, even.

When Matthew looks back to me, his expression has hardened.

"Well, I'm not anymore. And we need to find Serenity."

CHAPTER THIRTY
SERENITY

I want to yell, to scream, to fight.
Instead, I walk.

Or, more accurately, my body does. In reality,
I'm stuck on this damn island, too tired to even
move. I watch myself like my eyes are a movie,
but yelling at the screen will do nothing to keep
the heroin from walking into her doom.

I walk through the castle, deeper and deeper
until I think they're just going to kill me in the
dungeon.

Instead, though, they lead me through a cave,
the floor worn down from years of footsteps.

The walls are covered in slime, and the sound of the ocean crashes in my ears. If it were high tide, I'm certain this tunnel would be impassable.

When we hit the night air, my bare feet stinging from walking on sharp, uneven floors, I expect to find a boat. Instead, one of the men starts removing his clothes.

My heart doesn't even speed up.

He doesn't approach me like I expect from years of walking through the New York City streets defensively, though. Instead, he transforms, his body huge and brass, glinting in the gentle lights from the castle that stands high above us. The sky is covered in clouds, so there isn't a star in sight.

I don't react as a careful claw wraps around my body, although my head rushes when he takes to the air.

Matthew is gone.

Our connection is broken, and his body will rot in the earth if they don't burn it first.

Nothing matters.

I close my eyes and let the night take me.

Wherever they take me cannot be worse than the feeling that has hollowed out my heart and eviscerated my mind.

The fire that glows in my soul finally goes out.

To be continued...

*Keep reading for a preview of Dragon Hunted, book 2
in the Draecus Clan series!*

CHAPTER ONE
DYLAN

Death is nothing new to me.

When I was a baby, my mother died while holding me. So did my father.

Humans quickly learned that they needed to wear gloves to touch me.

I stalk through the palace, a rogue in the night. As invisible as one can be without magic. I approach the first rebel and lay my hand on his neck. Gently, almost like he's faking it, he sinks to the floor, his body lifeless. The energy of his life flows from my fingertips to my feet like an unstoppable river, and my throat that was parched a moment before has now been quenched. The relief is palpable.

I am good at killing because it feels good to kill. When I found out that Adrian killed a man in New York, fury raged through my body like a brushfire in a desert. It should have been me. Today, though, that fire is more than put out. I approach another, but he turns to me. Before he can open his mouth, my hand is upon him.

Dead.

Three men round the corner, and for a moment, I don't recognize them. My heart sings with excitement at the thought of *more, more, more.*

"Dylan," Matthew barks, and disappointment puts out the fire in my heart. I would never tell them that, of course. If they knew just how badly my soul wants to take life, they'd have me put away in the darkest, deepest dungeon, never to be seen again. Matthew's eyes flick to the stone floor, where the two men appear to be sleeping. The color hasn't even had time to drain from their cheeks.

I remember my exercises, breathing in through my nose and out through my mouth. The scent that falls upon me, though, is strange.

"What happened to you?" I ask, finally realizing that Matthew is covered in blood. There's some on Adrian as well, but not nearly as much. It's like Matthew decided to get baptized in red, or like someone bled out on top of him. I sniff again, and the stench of death hits me again, a power too strong to ignore.

"I died," he says, his jaw ticking. "It doesn't matter. Serenity has been taken. We need to—" My anger drowns out the rest of his words, and another group of men rounds the corner. When they see Matthew standing there, his body a scar in the otherwise desaturated hallway, their eyes fill with fear. Before they can convince themselves otherwise, though, they charge.

I slice through my friends, my team, like a shadow. With three tiny prods to the rebels' exposed skin, a waterfall of relief pours over me.

There's one left, though, and resolve settles in his eyes. I smile. The ones who try to live are the fun ones. The hunter in me is alive, and every body that falls adds fuel to the fire. *Another, another, another,* the beast calls.

"Dylan, stop," a woman's voice says. The command rings through me, and my body tenses up, the power draining away before I can even attempt to grasp at it.

Adrian, Matthew, and Dylan stalk past me and force the final rebel to the ground, and I have to suck in deep breaths to keep from feeling like I'm suffocating. It doesn't help much.

The queen glides past me, and the man on the ground does not struggle.

"My lady," he spits, his voice nothing but raw venom.

She smiles and tilts her head. Does he see the viciousness that lurks beneath?

"I could have you cut off your own fingers, you know," she says, her voice sickeningly sweet. The death I would give is a quick one, but what the queen can do is far worse. "But I will be kind enough to ask you first. Where have you taken my daughter?"

The man laughs, a short, hostile sound that has no humor in it. My breathing evens out, and I glare. I want so badly to kill him, but the queen's order, so filled with power, keeps me frozen in place like a statue.

"Fine," the queen says calmly. Then, with magic crackling in the air around her, she says, "Take the knife in your belt and cut out your left eye." She considers for a moment, then adds, "Slowly."

The man stares up at the queen, fear crossing his face as his left hand fumbles for the knife in its sheath. "Stop," he mumbles to himself, then tries to grab the hand with his other. Instead, his right hand takes the knife and turns it toward his face. I can do nothing but watch as the blade moves closer and closer, despite the man yelling "no!" repeatedly. When it's less than an inch from his eye, he screams, "Please! I'll talk!"

The queen waves a hand, and the command is released. The rebel drops the knife and kicks it away, his body shivering as he watches the weapon warily.

"Talk," Adrian says. We all know the queen could have just ordered him to tell us, which is why nausea now rolls in my gut. I've never seen her like this, not ever.

"She's on an island," he says. "You don't want to go there, though. There's a rebel stronghold. There are hundreds of dragons."

The queen tilts her head. "How long has this been going on?"

The man shivers. "I don't know, I swear. I was just brought in a few months ago." His voice is barely more than a whisper, the sound rasping out of him.

"Liam, is he telling the truth?" Amelie asks, her eyes not leaving the man's face. Liam's jaw is clenched, but he nods. He couldn't possibly be comfortable with this. He has the softest heart of us all. "And do you have a location?"

When the man's eyes widen, Liam nods again.

"Kill him quickly," the queen says, walking away with a frown. The words in themselves are not an order, but they seem to release me from the hold of her previous command. My hands shake.

"You don't have to do this," the man says, keeping his eyes on my hands. He knows exactly what I can do by now, the bodies of his comrades still strewn across the floor. His eyes turn golden from the sheer level of emotion coursing through his body.

"I know," I say.

Adrian refuses to make eye contact with me as I put my hand on the man's cheek.

ABOUT THE AUTHOR

ALEXIS PIERCE *is a small-town writer with a big-*city heart. She travels the world full time in search of a place to call home, and, when she's not writing about sexy supernatural creatures, can be found spending time with her husband and dogs.

Made in the USA
Monee, IL
03 August 2024

63218662R00142